Table of Contents

The Untamed Grassland

The Nasty Frostbite

Fight for the Aleutian Islands

Reminiscence

Pheasants in Peka for Christmas

The Giant Snakeskin

Another Day in the Cave

Raising Crops

A Sign on the Roof

A Brush with the Violent Side of Nature

Back to the Beginning

The Birthday Vacation

A Private Dinner

One Year Later

A Day at the Anchorage

Living to Fight Another Day

Battle of the Titans

Reincarnation So What Happened?

The Flaming Cottage

The Unbroken Pot

Waiting in Despair

Tears of a Mother

To Kaitlyn, Lilly B., Christian B., and Isaac Castleberry, Tulsa, Oklahoma, All Canossians, Dar Es Salaam Tanzania, and Jeremiah and Esther Ojera Awoii, Kampala, Uganda.

Acknowledgments

I am indebted to Chuck Charles from Page Publishing who continually checked on my progress month after month until I mailed him the manuscript. A thank you to Kendall Hyde for coordinating the publication process smoothly and answering all my questions promptly, plus her team of editors from Page Publishing for doing an excellent job.

Much appreciation to Isaac Okwir who did a fantastic work with the illustrations.

And finally, I am indebted to my wife, Annastazia Kimambo Awoii, who gave me a pass from my domestic chores so I could spend a few hours a day in the library to produce this work.

I am forever grateful.

PROLOGUE

It was a fine and beautiful sunny day with silky, bluish sky at noon in 1963 when it all started. The wind blew lightly, swirling Christina's curly hair as she stood gazing at the bronze Sakakawea statue on the state capitol grounds, Bismarck City, North Dakota. She was a student at the college there in the city and, being always fond of art, was enjoying the fine handiwork of Leonard Crunelle. Crunelle's work stood symbolically on the state capitol grounds, and it was undeniably a sight to see. Her blue jeans and white blouse matched the colors of the sky as though she had a date with the celestial realm on that spring day.

Beside her were two friends, all girls, dressed too casually for normal students—perhaps because it was a Friday afternoon with the weekend just around the corner. And for the teacher who had accompanied them to the brief sightseeing event, there was no better word than "perfect" to describe him when it came to his dress code. Mr. Logan, the science lecturer at the college, wore a light-blue long-sleeved shirt with moss-green necktie, a little bit rough texturally, contrasting the smoothness of his pair of gray pants. He wore no jacket, which gave him a student-like nature, being the middle-aged lecturer that he was. He and all the three students had an intersecting interest—appreciation of art. That was what prompted them to use the lunch break for the brief expedition. As they stood there, Mr. Logan seemed engrossed in explaining something to the three students as they focused their attention on the statute before them and occasionally looked at him as if to confirm the facts about the art piece that gallantly stood before them.

Having satisfied their eyes, they promptly walked toward Mr. Logan's light-blue Nash Rambler and headed off toward the campus.

"What about lunch, guys?" Miss Christina asked.

"I know what we can quickly do given the little time left," responded the teacher.

After that, they detoured and drove down the street to Kroll's Diner, ordered their burgers, and sat down for a quick meal before continuing to school. Mr. Logan, having offered to cover for lunch, walked up to the counter and placed a five-dollar bill on the counter, and they left hurriedly to catch up with the afternoon lectures. It was a successful trip. Being a new lecturer at the college, he was getting acquainted with the culture of the institution. There was much to learn from students as well as staff. It was his tenth time visiting the Capitol building to sightsee and learn.

They drove silently for a moment and soon arrived at the campus. He stopped at the parking lot so his passengers could hurry off to their respective lecture halls. Everyone said their thanks to each other and vanished among the buildings, leaving Mr. Logan who took a bit of time before he finally emerged from the car with his leather bag in hand and walked toward the staffroom.

In Bismarck city, tradition and culture stood as defining attributes to the Midwestern State of North Dakota, the land of the originals. Native Americans have inhabited the place for thousands of years, and up to about thirty thousand of them lived there then, making 5 percent of the total population of America. Earlier on, before the 1950s, the number was far less; but nonetheless, the culture then was even richer. "Dakota" literally meant—still does—allies or friends, a welcoming gesture to all. The students who studied in Bismarck College therefore had a thing about the symbolism of Bismarck standing as a reflection of the entire state by exhibiting cultural symbols and statues, which they took keen interests in appreciating and exploring.

Many indigenous tribes made up the whole body of Native Americans. From the Mandan, Hidatsa, Arikara, Hunkpapa, Dakotah, and Lakotaha, or the Sioux, all having a commonality of reverence for the earth and the understanding of mankind's relationship with nature and the spirits. The Natives were, and still are, strongly spiritual people. Even though most of the cities in the state had a strong presence of the culture and tradition of the locals, there were lots of other people of diverse backgrounds who had settled in the state after the arrival of Europeans who first settled in part of the Minnesota territory and then in Dakota Territory in the nineteenth century.

In the late 1950s, when Bismarck State College was establishing itself as one of the most prominent colleges in and around the capital city, Bismarck, Stephen Logan, a descendant from the early Europeans who settled there, found a teaching job in the department of biological sciences and was commuting from a nearby suburb of Lincoln, barely ten miles from the college. He was a middle-aged, career-driven gentleman and a family man.

* * *

The day was bustling and busy as he wrapped up his work at the college, ready for the long-awaited weekend. He quickly tidied up his work desk, removed a bioscience textbook from the leather bag, placed it on the desk, marked a page with a yellow wooden ruler, and left in a hurry so he could be home in time to continue with his storytelling obligation to his son, Larry Logan.

When it came to stories, it was part of a long-standing tradition going back to generations. The stories he'd heard about spirits, the folklore stories of Dakota—the land that he'd loved as a kid and as an adult—came handy when it finally dawned on him that it was his turn to share them with his son in order to preserve and continue the beautiful tradition and the way of life. Three times a week for them was story night, and they both looked forward to it as an opportunity for a father-and-son time after dinner. He obviously recognized how his son, Larry, had become so fond of the stories, and so he was happy they were doing it. He hoped Larry would carry on the tradition to his future grand and great-grandchildren.

Logan's work at the college was clearly becoming more demanding at the time, the reason being the spiking enrollment numbers due to the returning GIs from World War II. Despite that, he always kept their story date intact. And finally, he was home to shower and dine before they settled down to it. His son, Larry Logan, was waiting as usual.

Time check, and it was 9:15 p.m. There was a knock on his bedroom door. As expected, it was his father who walked in. Naturally, he was sleepy and yet not ready to close his eyes yet. It was story time, bedtime story, to be specific. His dad was a prolific storyteller. He had a bag full of them, and how deep that bag was, no one could tell. Larry had listened to his stories since he became conscious of who he was as a kid. He, however, didn't quite remember when that was.

The only thing he knew, though, was that he was twelve, a typical teenager already, and that his father's stories were getting even more and more complex every passing day. He was addicted to them. Sometimes he felt like the day wasn't going fast enough for the evening story time to finally come. Larry was a typical grade-seven kid with friends that he played with in the neighborhood and school. The only thing that was unique about him, though, was that he was a story fanatic. And his dad was to blame for that. Well, blame wasn't probably a good word to use in the normal sense, but since sometimes his friends called him a weirdo for loving stories more than sports, then maybe his dad's "act" could qualify him to be blamed.

Larry was addicted to his father's stories just the same way he was addicted to his mother's cooking. His mom, Mrs. Sylvia Logan, was a fantastic chef. She cooked all different kinds of traditional American recipes, exploring into the complicated Oriental dishes and the far Eastern European delicacies. Some of the recipes that she explored would take a day or two to put together. To Larry, that was a whole science: washing, marinating, deep-frying and draining oil, wrapping and baking, sometimes slow-cooking in the oven or crock-pot for hours. And before you finally served, you'd have gone through countless stages of cooking procedures. Larry loved lamb peka that originated from Croatia, Dalmatia region, for example. He thought he could eat it every day for a year. Of course, that was an example of childhood fanaticism and sometimes obsessions with fancy foods. As a commonality, all kids do that at some point. "I find my mom's style of cooking so fascinating, and that makes me want to become a chef in the future," Larry once told a friend next door.

He wanted to become a storyteller too. And by the looks of things, his father seemed to have made sure that happened in the future when Larry grew up. He was so consistent and dedicated to their bedtime story routine as though it was part of a school syllabus. He loved that Larry loved his stories, and that was inspiring to him. Larry loved his father too. It was their bonding time as dad and son.

For that night they were entering day two of a story that was as fascinating and scary at the same time. Throughout the day Larry had been ruminating over the myriad threads of the story that his dad had left hanging at many different levels.

Chapter One

THE UNTAMED GRASSLAND

The stage was set, and the story began miles away in another place—Alaska Territory, where the mountains and the caves stood out as defining signatures, not forgetting the fact that when it came to frigid temperatures, Alaska was a record holder as well. Temperatures in the excess of minus fifty degrees Fahrenheit below zero had happened there and continue to happen. Looking at the title, little Larry thought it was one of the spookiest he'd seen: *The Devil in the Cave*.

"Really, wow!"

Larry couldn't wait to resume!

When they settled down to it, his father sat on the bedside and asked, "So, where were we?"

"The hunter and Gossiper were out hunting, and they'd just spotted a pair of deer," Larry responded.

"Yep, you're right," his dad replied.

And so, it continued that Gossiper vanished into the thickets on the side of the walk path and, suddenly there was a rattling noise, like strong wind surging through the shrubby bush nearby.

* * *

It was daybreak, and the morning sun answered to its promise of a new day, sending its piercing rays through the shadowy grassland at the break of dawn. Archibald got up from his game-hide bed, looked up at the dimly lit ceiling of his tiny makeshift, red-roofed cottage. He could hardly see anything yet. He yawned satisfactorily as he rubbed his right eye with the back of his hand, and then the left eye as if to balance the equation of his commitment to both for their equal service.

He squinted as he frantically focused his view to the ceiling, blinking rapidly and now trying hard to make out where his stick toothbrush was stuck the previous morning. There! He found it. A pen-sized branch of acacia plant was blending with the uniformly lined bamboo faggots used to thatch the roof from the inside.

He reached out to the fireplace by the door on his way out and took a piece of charcoal that had survived the evening ember that simmered while he laid down the night before. He tapped it lightly on the unburned wood like a cigarette smoker, shaking off the ashes from the tip of a burning cigar so he could expose the real black charcoal within.

Stepping out, he squatted by the door side, looked at the piece of charcoal in his left hand, and, as if it was a piece of candy, bit through it and chewed it into a black paste, blackening his mouth, tongue, and teeth as if he was sipping black paint. Ironically, his mouth freshened up in taste as he started brushing with the stick toothbrush. Back and forth for about a minute, he spat out the black paste on the ground and brushed again. He went back in for the rinsing water, scooped some in his brownish-yellow calabash, and cleansed his face, and he was almost ready. He rinsed his mouth twice, and his once-black mouth and teeth were clean and glistening.

He whistled sharply to Gossiper as though he was a village lad, beckoning to a local belle in the countryside. Gossiper was his beloved German shepherd, medium-sized and about sixty pounds; brown for the most part and blackish around the ears and mouth area. He was more than just an ordinary dog. For five years they'd been inseparable. He was like a son, a brother, and a friend, well-trained and sharp in all ways a dog could possibly be. Within ten seconds he heard faggots breaking in the distance as Gossiper galloped over the morning dew in evenly paced leaps toward his master. He was answering to the call, "Come on, boy, come on." Archibald rubbed Gossiper's neck as he wagged his dewy tail from side to side and growled as though he was saying a morning greeting to his master.

The sun's heat was reaching down more and more, and it was another promising day in the Susitna Valley. Archibald went back into the cottage, took his skin hunting pouch and scanned inside to ensure all the vital contents were intact. Even though he lived alone—well, save, of course, for his loyal friend, Gossiper, who would never distort or fish out anything from his bag—the quick search was a tradition he would have to live with as a code forever. It was pretty much like a preflight checklist that pilots go through routinely before the plane ever left the ground. Life and death it was, as a matter-of-fact.

Just like for the pilots, to him too, it was a matter of life and death in case one of the items in the bag was missing. He still recalled one incident with a shudder that sent cold chills down his spine every time he thought of it. It was there in Matanuska, during a regular fishing expedition down in the Little Susitna River. He had made big catches and was on his way back home when four giant moose, startled by a wild cat perhaps, emerged from nowhere in a nearby bush, running toward him in a frenzied mini stampede like soldiers charging at an adversary! Like the moose, he too was startled and, in the rush of adrenaline, stumbled over and got entangled by creeping vegetation. Before he knew it, he'd tumbled over the horsetail bushes along his path in the process of trying to get away, his legs firmly trapped! Thinking fast, like a soldier that he was, he quickly reached inside his life-saving kit, the hunting pouch, to dig out a knife and sever off the tantalizing vegetation that held him captive right in front of the surging moose.

"What!" he screamed! There wasn't any knife!

In a state of fury and desperation, there wasn't anything he could do to free himself. He was right there on the path of death, waiting for his ribs to be trampled on by the moose, crushed, and possibly killed. He helplessly laid there, bewildered. In the seconds that followed, he wondered how he had forgotten to put back the handy weapon, the knife, into the pouch after flaying his deer the previous evening. As thoughts ran through his foggy mind, Gossiper had assessed the murky situation of his master, ducked right in front of the moose with his master behind him, risking his life in the process, and barked frantically as he could and luckily warded off the attacking animals to a different direction!

Archibald was perplexed, relieved, and grateful he had a dog so keen and brave; so intelligent, almost like a human.

"How could I ever thank Gossiper?" he quietly asked himself as he tried to suppress the train of thoughts that ran through his mind.

With his focus back and clear, he got out the ten-inch knife with strong steely, silvery blade and wooden handle, which he mostly used for flaying and put it back inside. He then checked his battle-for-survival knife, a thirteen-inch long, steely blade welded firmly to a heavy metallic handle. Next he reached for his precious little five-inch oblong-shaped sharpening stone, which he used to keep his knives up to date. Capping it all, there were the two rubbing sticks, a fire-starting alternative in case the regular matches failed after getting wet accidentally. He also kept a sixteen-ounce fluid pouch for his water. After that, he was ready to hit the path.

He finally reached out for his most formidable weapon, the arrow, took the bow and the leather quiver—inside of which he kept eleven arrows. As a rule, he could only use ten. The last one was for survival and was only meant to be used for defensive purpose, literally the last arrow he'd ever shoot before dying if it ever came to it. With that, the preflight, or should we call it the pre-hunting, check was done and over. He was ready.

He popped out of the house; Gossiper stretched his entire body as he lowered his belly a few inches off the ground, throwing his forelegs forward as if he was a goalkeeper reaching for a soccer ball. Archibald whistled the hunting signal to Gossiper, and he knew exactly what they were up to. Different whistles meant different things and/or activities. For example, a long, sustained whistle meant hunting. Short whistles in three consecutive bursts meant fishing. You'd be amazed if you were still wondering if Gossiper actually knew those signals and their respective meanings.

Once he'd whistled them off to go fishing, and as they walked off, just a minute later when he looked back, Gossiper had vanished; and as soon as he whistled to call him from wherever he was, which was one long whistle followed by a three-second pause then a short whistle and repeated in the same fashion, Gossiper had reemerged from the direction of the cottage, and he couldn't believe what he saw. He'd returned to the cottage to retrieve the fishing float container, which he'd forgotten in the house!

Seeing that, he'd put down his bag, rubbed his back, telling him, "Good job, good job, boy," and Gossiper knew how proud his master was of him.

That was the last time he'd ever doubted what Gossiper was capable of. He was a freaking genius.

As they continued down the path, his mind wandered from one item to the next. He refocused back on the walk, pranced forward hurriedly through the dewy grassland, with Gossiper leading the way, his ears raised in a V-shape fashion like a double-network router antenna, as though he was collecting signals. And indeed, he was collecting signals. The fierce quick walk continued as if they were late for an appointment, and yet Archibald himself knew that in the jungle; he was in charge, and time was under his control. He didn't answer to anyone. Despite that, he knew one thing: it was easier to trap and chase the wild animals in the morning when the dew was dense and heavy on the grass blades. He took advantage of that.

As he paced along, on his mind was the thought of enjoying a nice, tasty venison soup, simmered and eaten with hot potatoes. As if the gods of the untamed grassland were listening to his inner thoughts, a pair of deer, startled by Gossiper, who'd dashed off from the walk path into a nearby shrubby bush, ran right in front of him, fifty yards perhaps. Instinctively he plucked an arrow from the quiver and aimed at the hind deer, following its speed for a few seconds, held his breath slowly as he released the weapon… Whoosh! He hit his target, the rib cage close to the forelimbs, and it tumbled over. Mission accomplished! It had taken them approximately seventeen minutes before they got the huge breakthrough of the day.

Chapter Two

THE NASTY FROSTBITE

L iving in isolation alone was enough challenge. His only cottage in the vast expanse of uninhabited land was like a tiny speck in the snowcapped mountainside of Alaskan territory. Looking at his orange-brown tiled roof from above, it was like a huge piece of brown leaf patched on the tapered greenery that uniformly embraced the landscape at the base of the greyish snowy mountain ranges. That was the life Archibald had chosen for himself. And since his wife-to-be passed on, he knew he was in it alone—alone like the yetis of the great Himalayan mountain ranges, secluded from the vibrant world teeming with people. At least he chose to only make the most of it as much as he could. That was his consolation, and there was no turning back from his primary decision now.

Approximately seven years ago he could've chosen to trek downhill toward Anchorage City and rejoin civilization and settle among the people, but instead in the process of mourning the loss of his beloved soulmate, he found himself reluctant to backtrack into normalcy, and so he just stayed. And then he stayed much longer. And the long-term plan was to stay more. He also purposely abandoned some basic practices. He preferred using naturally available materials to survive. He rarely used normal toothpaste and brushes. Sometimes whenever he ran out of soap and was reluctant to return to the Anchorage for supplies, he'd make some from the locally available materials. It worked for him. So far so good, so he thought.

Despite the solitude, he felt lucky and grateful to the gods to be alive at least and more so then with Gossiper who'd made his life way better and more meaningful. At all times he was always just a whistle away. Five years in it together and counting, off the grid and happy. He had food, which he produced in his small farm; plus he had water nearby and all he ever needed for survival. Everything he consumed was purely organic, and his weight and health were always constant and perfect. He was happy, he and Gossiper.

Besides his successes, there were challenges that he faced. Winter, for example, made things very compounded. He had to grudgingly prepare for it annually because there wasn't any choice. The frigid cold was unforgiving in the mountain region. Temperatures could plunge to a crazy -50 °F! Despite that, he was a proven survivalist and was always ready for the challenge. He was a soldier once, and his life in isolation demanded every experience he'd acquired over the years when he was in active duty.

It was mid-December, and the Christmas spirit was surging in the civilized regions of Alaska with the Christian settlements and the population generally readying for the climax of the festive season. There were the usual frenzy and the fast-paced shopping with fancy holiday presents crisscrossing the territory's road networks like particles in a colloidal state. And then there were little kids dreaming of white Christmas, with snowflakes gracing the chilly atmosphere on Christmas Eve. Others were expecting to prove whether Santa had really heard their secret requests for the season and if he was going to fulfill them. Perhaps the arrival of the presents they'd secretly requested for would act as proof of his divinity, or better still, his utter existence at all.

Curiosity and excitement were swirling all at once on the young minds as they earnestly checked off each day from the December calendar. To them, winter wasn't a threat. Instead it was an exciting moment with a different set of activities to be enjoyed. Skiing and building the snowman in the front yard were part of the game. Visiting Santa and getting cuddled in his arms were cool moments to look forward to as well. Great expectations awaited.

But approximately fifteen miles up from the banks of Susitna River in Matanuska, the story was different. Winter presented challenges beyond compare. For Archibald, winter required painstakingly methodical planning and preparations. It was about survival for the fittest. And he was a proven survivalist. He had seven years under his belt as solid proof in his résumé to make it through the wildest circumstances that unfortunately never ceased to present themselves in the Alaskan mountainside. Nonetheless, some credit had to be attributed to Gossiper who'd proven almost indispensable as a team player and partner in the survival game.

Like many days of clear chilly December skies, it was exactly four days to Christmas as Archibald could recall. In his mind he wished he was still working at Anchorage Hotel, where things were very different. There he'd be in the middle of Christmas performances, ushering in guests from all around Alaska and the mainland and enjoying the performances that were spectacular to say the least. A smile flashed across his face as he recalled all the beauty and splendor. It was just beautiful.

But down at the River Valley, he and Gossiper were going through their humble, strategic preps to cross into the New Year. January always presented the craziest days in the area, and they needed to get everything right as they headed into the final days of the year. Having gathered the charcoal from the unburned wood from a nearby forest and packed in straw bags, it was time to go across the frozen, glassy, icy Susitna River and bring the fresh wooden planks that he burned for housewarming and cooking during the winter months. The fresh woods burned slowly and for long hours and are thus suitable for the winter.

The process of harvesting those fresh woods had always been precise and safe. That wasn't to say that it was any easy; on the contrary, it was extremely delicate. Walking on the surface of a frozen river wasn't for the faint of heart. It was a meticulously maneuvered exercise at every level. After placing his red jacket on the grass at the riverside and leaving Gossiper waiting, he got to it.

As his common practice, Archibald did the first phase by successfully walking across and chopping two long logs into fifteen pieces, each roughly thirteen inches in diameter and three feet in length, then splitting them with his axe and machete. He had to consider the weight of each piece, given the fact he himself weighed approximately 165 pounds, and according to his simple physics, he didn't want the total weight exceeding 180 pounds each time he carried a plank across the icy river. You've probably already guessed correctly the consequences of making any tiny errors while performing the task. That was like one of those tasks of an aeronautic engineer, which they said no mistake was allowed.

To an aeronautic engineer, if you made one mistake, it'd be over. You wouldn't have another chance since the explosive would have finished you the first time.

And so Archibald carefully walked back and forth with each piece, one at a time sticking to the rule not to carry overweight. He did this for twenty-one laps as he labored to get finished up with the total of thirty pieces. On the twenty-second lap as he walked back, wooden plank held against his right shoulder, he accidentally slipped, dropping the plank on the surface; and as expected, the glassy ice went quack, quack! The hydrogen bonds that held the molecular crystals in the ice structures gave way, and there were enormous cracks that originated from the landing spot; and in a matter of seconds, Archibald was swallowed into the giant man-sized hole that opened on the clear, crystalline river.

The whole thing came as a surprise, like a hit on the back of the head by a silent killer. The water was probably twenty degrees Fahrenheit, which was well below the freezing temp of thirty-two degrees. Archibald felt the stinging frigidness on his bare skin, pervading his entire being as though he was stung by a swarm of bees at once. He tried to swim out, but the icily caked surface didn't make it any easier. He fumbled on, pausing momentarily to break the rest of the ice to clear his path as he swam to the shore.

He clearly spent longer trying to get out than one would've in clear waters—one and half minutes, perhaps, and that was a mighty long time. When he finally made it out, his teeth clattered in his mouth like rattlesnakes in a competing musical duel. He labored a whistle to Gossiper then started off heading to the cottage to set the emergency fire to warm up. His skin pricked him in a nasty frostbite that he was trying so hard to assuage.

He fanned the fire and spread his ten fingers over it like a priest praying over a crowd of confessors. Instinctively he went on rubbing his hands together occasionally, as if to supplement the heat of the fire with the frictional rub. Gradually the clattering of his teeth subsided, and he'd just survived a nasty frostbite from a nasty plunge into the frozen river.

Once he was fully recovered and ready to eat, he served his trout soup that he'd made with spicy jalapeño and potatoes. He served Gossiper in his plastic bowl, and he gulped it down in a minute. The scare of that night reminded him of the battle for the Aleutian Islands almost ten years ago when they fought the Japanese in Attu Island. It was similar, but not even close to the rough situations there; and so like he'd promised himself back then, he was going to treat the incident just like a little cold and frigid weather.

Chapter Three

FIGHT FOR THE ALEUTIAN ISLANDS

Many years ago, almost a decade when Archibald Arthur was barely nineteen, at a time when he was looking for an opportunity to make a difference and serve his country, a war broke out close to home. It coincided with a time in his life as a young man when he wanted to do something honorable, something he could be proud of later in life. And so, when the Japanese attacked Pearl Harbor on December 7, 1941, Hawaiian Territory, the United States was fully drawn into the war and so was Archibald Arthur.

At that point he knew he finally got his clear chance. It happened so fast and spontaneously, and without thinking of it, he was enlisted for training in the military. He recalled how he had to write just a single-lined letter to his parents to notify them of his decision and whereabouts saying, *"I am gone to the military!"*

That must've been the briefest letter he'd ever written yet. It was delivered three days after he was gone. He made sure his childhood buddy, Ian, delivered it after his father couldn't find him and try to persuade him not to join the military. That was his big chance to do something for his country. Even though at the time Alaska was technically still a United States' territory looking forward to attain statehood, Archie was sold out, knowing Alaska would soon become a part of the mainland. That made defending the Alaskan Territory against the Japs even more patriotic to him. By the time he enrolled, the Japanese had aggressively poked the United States in the eye more times than any other country so far. They had bombed Midway, which further dented the morale of the American troops. It was therefore imperative to recapture the Aleutian Islands, which were strategically placed and paramount for effective military operation of the United States. In 1943 the war intensified, and Archibald was in the middle of it, his unit having been tasked alongside their Canadian combatants to retake the islands. They jointly mounted a frantic battle and pushed to reclaim the islands.

Despite the rough and dangerous terrain of Attu and Kiska islands, it was more about their strategic value that the United States couldn't afford to allow any enemy forces to get a hold of. In the words of General Billy Mitchel of the US Army to Congress earlier in 1935, he had said, "Whoever holds Alaska will hold the world." The Americans feared that the islands could be used as launching pads to a full-scale attack on the mainland. Archibald was a young recruit who, together with his colleagues, understood that point perfectly. The stakes were so high, and they were ready to give their lives for the country if it came to it. For many it became the ultimate sacrifice.

* * *

That morning the unit commander addressed them and assured them that whatever they were doing was far bigger and greater than each one of them individually.

"Each man with his rifle, and yet together we function as a unit with many revolving parts. We rise and fall together and will stick to the training that we've received and fight with courage for our great nation. By the fact that you have sacrificed your time and life to serve our people, you are heroes of the American people. That's it, boys—heroes—and don't you ever forget that," their unit commander shouted as he winded his speech, and right at that moment gunfire erupted and rocked the rugged terrain like sesame seeds being roasted in a cooking pan.

Immediately we started advancing and making the final push to reclaim Attu Island; there was no going back. It was life and death. We could hear air support approaching in the distance. As I looked up, I saw six PBY, the World War II Catalina warplanes flying toward the enemy battle line in a V-shape formation. The engines rumbled deafeningly as they flew directly overhead. Within seconds we could see them spitting fire as bombs rained down on Japanese tents that we could faintly see through the foggy morning over the hills on the other side. Giant tongues of flames leaped up each time a bomb met the earth on the enemy side.

We felt a sigh of relief. However, that feeling soon disappeared when we realized that we were going down there to clean up the mess after the aerial bombardments were over. But it was our duty, and we were prepared to go searching.

The next five days that followed were the most challenging in my entire military career. We hiked inch by inch toward the garrisons of the outnumbered Japanese soldiers who'd retreated to the higher grounds. The mission which was dubbed "Operation Landgrab" ended up taking two weeks, which proved to be the longest ever. We walked into the wildest weather one could think of. Frostbite, gangrene, unbridled hunger, fatigue due to the rugged, muddy terrain were beyond compare. The frigid conditions proved more devastating than the Japanese gunfire.

As we advanced deeper and deeper, we encountered more fighters who would open fire each time we got closer to their garrisons. We'd return fire and proceed cautiously, but relentlessly. Around 2:00 p.m. in the afternoon that day, things got even weirder when the wild weather made it look like it was nightfall due to poor visibility. The fogginess blanketed the island as though the clouds had come down to mate with the earth and never to rise up again. We could barely see anything beyond a hundred yards.

As we inched forward, gunfire erupted suddenly in the frontline, and I heard a scream from one of my buddies, one, Jackson Wyatt.

"I am hit, I am hit," he shouted.

He fell into the muddy trenches created by erosion in the isolated island as he moaned. I darted toward him, held his hand, and saw blood oozing from a fresh wound on his left thigh. I quickly removed a tourniquet and a chunk of cotton wool from my backpack and got to work. I placed the cotton wool directly over the wound and tied it tightly to control the bleeding. By now the gunfire was deafening, but I continued with the rescue mission. I lifted my friend up shoulder to shoulder, and we staggered toward the base while holding my rifle with the left hand just in case. A plane flew in the distance and dropped a couple of bombs away as he could see. That gave him assurance that the Air Force had them covered. Thirty minutes later he had carried his friend half the way to safe zone. He got the much-needed medical attention. He looked at my face feebly and said a faint "thank you." I responded with a thumbs-up and headed back to the front line.

We were trained never to leave a fellow combatant behind no matter what. It was a code of brotherhood that we all lived by.

As I jogged back to the frontline, I heard another plane fly overhead, this time very close by, and like before dropped a few bombs, followed by retaliatory artillery gunfire from the Japanese occupiers roughly a mile down from our location. We continued ahead.

The Japs fought wildly and fiercely to the very end. But with supply lines cut off from them by the American Navy and Air Force, there was no way out of Attu by the trapped Japs. From there I learned how to survive, and given what we went through, I said to myself that any ordinary conditions back home wouldn't be insurmountable to me anymore should we survive the carnage. The worst weather conditions on earth! It was estimated that only eight days in a year were without rain, fog, snow, or sleet! That was some classic williwaws not found anywhere on the planet. We prayed to make it out of that horrific battle—the only battle on American soil during World War II. Finally, the heavens heard us, and there was the silver lining. The remaining pockets of the Japs made their final push, and that was when they hit the last snag. Depleted of ammunitions and basic supplies, they opted for mass suicide instead of surrendering as POWs to the unrelenting American and Canadian troops.

It was the end of the road for them and a new beginning for

us. The lucky ones among us made it back, and I later retired from active service and started a new chapter of my life as a civilian and a vet. In November the same year, 1943, Archibald was back home for a break. He had returned from active service after the battle for the Aleutian Island was concluded in August with the Japs cleared from the arena. His evaluation: he was satisfied with his participation and what he'd accomplished.

After that, he was confronted with a decision to make. And before he could get to it, he sought advice from the recruiting office and weighed his options: either to retire or remain in active service. He chose the former; he was laying down the weapon and going into civilian life full swing. He was ready to turn the page and begin a new chapter. Even though the battle had left irrefutable aftereffects, he was ready to rediscover himself. Post-traumatic stress disorder was his number one fear. He'd gone through tough stuff there in the frontline and seen so much carnage, but he was ready to face his fears and giants and conquer them one after another. He was sure to put the ordeal behind him. And so, he sought counselling and diligently attended sessions for months. He also set his sights in working in hotel industry, especially as a security guard. He had several job leads already within the Anchorage area, and as soon as he was stable enough, he was going to flood his applications around.

Chapter Four

REMINISCENCE

As far back as he could recall, it was June 1951, and Archibald had just celebrated his twenty-ninth birthday that came fresh in his memory. After the flames from the embers of World War II had died down and cooled off, the United States' economy was on a positive trajectory, and the economic prosperity was steadily coming through and becoming more prevalent in the land. Things were looking better and promising.

Most of the adults, including Archibald at the time, were born and raised during the great depression of the 1930s, which saw the worst destitution in the history of the republic. More to that, there was the additional dent left by the war that the populace had lived through and still recovering from. Despite all that, President Harry Truman's policy of implementation of the Marshall Plan of rebuilding Europe's economy to counter the Soviet Union's geopolitical ambitions of expansionism at the onset of the Cold War was proving successful and as well boosting domestic growth.

Accompanying the progress made by that historically renowned American foreign policy of countering and containing Soviet expansion, which consequently led to the birthing of North Atlantic Treaty Organization, the simultaneous rollout of universal health care and the raising of minimum wage led to spectacular economic boom. The result was an economic growth at a remarkable rate of 14.2 percent, according to the World Economic Report. That economic boom translated into a freer, richer, and more willing population to purchase and spend. One of the prominent outcomes was an uptick in performance of the hotel industry in the country. The other equally vital consequence was an upsurge in the population. In the Territory of Alaska, for example, there was an astronomical leap in population growth.

With business booming and Anchorage Hotel's profile steadily rising across the territory, as well as nationwide, Anchorage was enjoying a renewed spotlight. Having been revamped about a decade ago, it was time for prominence. That wasn't the only silver lining; the population of Anchorage City climbed in leaps and bounds from a bare under five thousand to almost fifty thousand in the 1950s, and that ensured a widened customer base for the hotel business in the city. The future was bright, and Rosette Candy, the front desk supervisor, could see that. They were receiving guests from all corners of Alaska and nationwide. Stunningly, international guests were also becoming frequent arrivals in the hotel, and that made things even better for the hotel.

* * *

December 1950. On the front gate of Anchorage Hotel hung a fabric banner that read, "Live Christmas Festival Tonight." The second line on the strip said, "Come One, Come All, and See Real Talent." The Hotel Complex stood with glamor and a symbolic display of class. It was one of the tallest structures in the Anchorage downtown area in the 1950s. Anchorage's profile was attributed to high-profile individuals both from the American society, plus international bigwigs and businesspersons who'd trodden the corridors of the hotel. Simply put, it was a dwelling place for "the crème de la crème." It was like the rich man's palace. No wonder Warren Gamaliel Harding, the twenty-ninth president of the United States, spent nights there in the early 1920s. Walt Disney and Will Rogers, too, were frequent guests.

Besides the big names, the quality of the services and entertainment offered to the guests gave additional credence and novelty to the arena. It was a place to be. When Archibald retired from active service, he admired working there, and he got his chance.

For countless nights, Archibald Arthur, the chief security officer at the hotel, had coordinated meticulous security detail with government officials, and he'd lost count. On those "live band" nights, or during the Christmas festivals, the challenges they had dealt with were extraordinary. But their main goal was always to balance between maintaining the safety of the high-profile guests who rubbed shoulders at the facility and at the same time promoting the vibrant culture of the hotel and keeping it lively for guests of all walks of life.

One of those memorable nights Archibald recalled how he had to arrange for his security team to wear three sets of uniforms, which had to be changed after every two to three hours. They would shuffle and send written coded messages to initiate a change to another color, which would take five minutes, and all the guards would be in a different uniform.

* * *

As James Russel, a security officer who was dressed as a waiter and working undercover for the team that night, passed by with a shiny silver tray in his left hand and bottle of fake wine as he walked into the back corridor of the hotel and headed toward the VIP lounge, he met with a guard who wore a silky blue uniform who turned around and headed toward the same direction. Immediately Russel knew the guard was an impostor, since the blue uniforms were changed six minutes ago before he started his routine patrol of the VIP lounge area and the corridors. Before he could decide what to do, a guest emerged from the far corner, coming from one of the rooms, and spoke to them both in some European accent; sounded like French accent. Russel quickly told the guest that he had a message for him from the front desk. He asked the impostor guard on blue uniform to hold for him the tray and requested him to help return the tray back to the reception area. The impostor was compelled to oblige in order not to blow his cover, and by the time he got close to the reception area, Russel had informed three of the nearest officers and the intruder was apprehended.

It turned out the assassin was targeting an ambassador from Columbia. And after the assassination attempt was foiled, the hotel was dubbed to be with the "tightest security devoid of leak" by diplomats and government officials who frequented the place. That meant more business and progress for the hotel.

Archibald had been on the job for almost five years and was the most senior guard at the hotel. He knew the protocols and was excellent at his job. He had come face-to-face with dignitaries and international big shots from across the globe. He'd met musicians, artists, evangelists, and a multitude of women of class. In his job, it was like walking a fine line between civility and work ethic. Luckily, he'd kept his cool as well as his job. That same week there were new arrivals from Eastern Europe. Tourists perhaps, Archibald had thought to himself. He later learned that one of the ladies was Croatian, and the rest of the guests were British. He had welcomed and helped them to settle in their rooms. Most of the transatlantic travelers stayed longer at the facility, and he'd hoped they did. He particularly liked the young lady who settled in Room 24, but that was just about it. He went on and finished his day and clocked out of the shift and left.

Chapter Five

PHEASANTS IN PEKA FOR CHRISTMAS

Having put the incident of the frostbite behind him, Archibald capped his preparation for Christmas by putting together all his ingredients to make his favorite recipe as part of his unbreakable holiday tradition. He'd done that every Christmas since his wife passed on. To him, it was a time to harmonize with the entire world outside of the River Valley and celebrate the summit of the holiday season. It was about sharing the happiness with the world. More so, he would be cooling off and relaxing from the tedious work he'd done lately, prepping for the final winter push. It was so far so good.

To celebrate that, he was cooking peka as his top-on-the-menu delicacy. Peka was one of the lasting legacies that his wife had left him with almost eight years ago. Matilda, for that was her name, had learned the art from her father, Mr. Andreas Juergen, who was born in the Frankfurt area, Germany, where he had met her mother years ago while she was vacationing there. She was from Croatia. Her parents fell in love, and the two agreed to make it work. He later followed her to Croatia where they got married and started a family. It was there that Matilda's dad learned to cook while working as a chef in a local pizzeria, which served many popular dishes including peka. That was almost a decade ago.

Two years later into their life together, she was born. At a tender age of four, Matilda discovered her love for peka; and by age nine, she could make perfect peka, plus several other recipes. She was a little genius in her own way. When fate brought her and Archibald together in Alaska years ago, it was like history was repeating itself in her own life, falling in love while vacationing in a foreign country, like it happened to her parents. While on that fateful vacation in the United States, the very first time Archibald met her, he knew it wasn't going to be a short-term friendship. They stuck together, and the rest, as they say, is history.

Now that he thought about it, and how she had insisted on teaching him how to cook all kinds of recipes and especially peka, he couldn't thank her enough. It was funny that back then he had to be forced to oblige when he couldn't stand her nagging anymore. After she was gone, it was a different story, and he would thank her with tears rolling down his cheeks if he could ever get a chance. Peka was the real deal.

During his mourning, he had thought long and hard about what he could do in his dilemma that she was gone and decided to make cooking peka part of a lasting memory held tightly close to his heart as a permanent sign of his love. And, taking it up a notch, whenever he prepared the meal, he'd serve a second plate and set it beside his plate, along with a cup of Locale drink, which he'd leave there for hours after he'd finished his meal and finally throw it into the backyard, down into the earth as a sign of service to her. Given the expansive recipe of peka, he would use improvised ingredients as substitutes for the unavailable ones in his solitary abode. Pheasant was his meat of choice to begin with. He could use lamb or venison sometimes, but his favorite was the pheasant.

With his goal set for the grand meal on Christmas Eve, he went hunting for the American pheasants two miles away from the cottage. Gossiper, his "hunting buddy", knew exactly how he wanted it done; and so after arriving at the area, he ran around the bush, tracking their scent while wagging his tail to indicate he smelled something. They worked together like a perfect team. Gossiper was like a setter in a volleyball or basketball team, and he, Archibald, was the finisher as well as the slam dunker. And he was such a nasty slammer at that.

The tracking built up into a crescendo and melodrama as Gossiper rushed after the birds. All indications showed they were close, and in a sudden, startling clapper of multiple wings, five pheasants rose from under the shrubby grassland yards away. In rapid sequence that lasted about fifteen seconds, Archibald was able to down two of the birds in two successive arrow shots before they veered off behind the bush. That was all he needed: one for Christmas Eve and the other for the twenty-fifth of December itself. He liked cooking it fresh, but at least for just one night he'd preserve the second bird with salt and hang it over the fireplace overnight. They hurried home so Archibald could wrap up his cooking for the day.

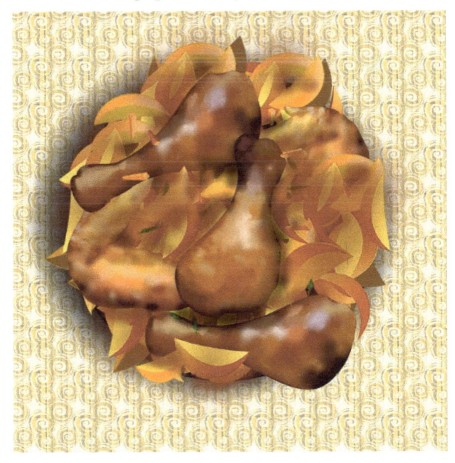

First, he boiled water, dipped the pheasants one at a time, and plucked off the feathers with ease. He did the same with the other and cleaned then chopped out into pieces. He salted the other and put it away. Fresh potatoes chopped into sizeable pieces, fresh zucchini from his farm, cleaned and chopped. Carrots chopped into two-centimeter segments. Instead of olive oil, he used vegetable oil, which was readily available, and he still had some in supply. Salt and pepper measured and added. Onion chopped into eight pieces and added to the mix. He massaged the mixture and placed it in his clay pot, and set it in the middle of the burning coals, and covered with a huge dish-shaped tin, or peka, and cooked it under low temperatures for about an hour, then opened it and flipped the chopped meat and potatoes to avoid the burning. After another hour, it was completely done, and he and Gossiper had a feast in unison with the rest of the world on this happy holiday evening. He enjoyed Locale and served some for the spirit of his departed wife-to-be, and he was happy. He went to bed satisfied of all they had done and was ready for the final lap of the season.

His Christmas in the jungle was simple enough, not like at the hotel then. A stream of thoughts ran through his mind as he reminisced the past—one memorable Christmas that he enjoyed there and wouldn't forget.

* * *

The main hall was packed to capacity that evening, and the stage was set for a historic Christmas festival at Anchorage Hotel. There were prominent guests of varying ranks down to the common townsfolks, the elite and semi-elite all converged in the magnificent arena to enjoy a beautiful Christmas and the season.

Within the confines of the soundproofed hall, the melody of the traditional Christmas song, *Silent Night*, graced the expectant atmosphere as the organizers of the event zeroed on the final details of the program, which was scheduled to kick off in a little under fifteen minutes. Immediately it clocked 8:00 p.m. the green velvety canopy on stage cracked opened from the middle section, and as it rolled back, the golden section also folded backward toward the light sky-blue walls. A giant Christmas tree stood in the background, laced with a bunch of golden, silvery ornaments that sent twinkling lights and sparkles against the backdrop of magnificent stage lighting that swirled the stage as though it was a discotheque arena. It was awesome.

Two gentlemen and ladies stood still in the center and, as soon as the curtains stopped rolling, burst into an opening song, singing a version of the newly released song, *Frosty the Snowman*. The song pierced into the quietly packed arena like trumpets from the sky on the last day, conveying the full effect to the ecstatic crowd; and as soon as the last notes rang off, there was a spontaneously thunderous applause from the now-electrified audience, drunk with the spirit of Christmas.

One performance after another the singers never stopped wowing the crowd. There was a ballet dance in the middle of the show that was so spectacular there was a standing ovation that lasted for a minute and initiated donations to be put in the basket by grateful spectators. Thereafter came a guitar soloist. At 10:00 p.m. the two-hour long show came to a close. Some of those moments made Archibald realize that being a guard wasn't easy. Still in the wonderland of his own thoughts, he recalled how difficult it was, standing at the concert gate while excitement brewed inside the hall to the pinnacle. That was hard. Sometimes he'd felt like wanting to be in two places at the same time—at the entrance to the concert hall and right in the middle of the show—spectating and feasting on the beautiful performance. Because of that, they had designed their little schedules where they'd take turns in and out for thirty-minute intervals. It was the only way. That was his Christmas to remember. He shook his head and had to let it go for now. It was in the past.

Chapter Six

THE GIANT SNAKESKIN

The remaining part of the winter came and went fast, and the temperatures climbed steadily into the fifties as they headed toward late March. After a little while it was time to look out for the American robin, the harbinger of warm, pleasant weather. The dwellers around the vicinity of the Alaskan mountainside were finally stepping out of a bitter winter and were super ready to put it all behind them and embrace the nice, sunny weather again.

One of those fine days, as always, Gossiper was ahead of Archibald and almost running, ears in the usual V-shape as they trekked toward the *Valley of Death*. Archibald would never forget the experiences he'd had there over the years: a gloomy, scary path with an aura of bad omen to it, the atmosphere tense with the macabre of death and panic that lightened your head as if in anticipation of a terrible thing about to happen.

It was there that his fiancée was killed, and it was an awful experience like nothing he would want to go through again. That was over five years ago. As he remembered the graphic details of the event, he couldn't help but shudder. For that, he'd nicknamed the place the *Valley of Death*. It was spooky and stinking with the acrid stench of fungal molds and rotting flesh, which you couldn't figure out where it was coming from. To make it worse, the narrow pathway led straight down into a densely forested moorland that swallowed hikers who dared against the odds to go in there, like divers disappearing into a blue sea. And for the Valley of Death, even though the temperature wasn't too cold outside, the densely forested cave mouth was as cold as winter. Within minutes he and Gossiper were swallowed up into the forest and about to arrive at the mouth of the giant cave, and at that moment, every step they took felt as though they were walking down an abyss into a realm from which they'd never return. It was that feeling that had kept Archibald from ever venturing into the cave. At least for close to seven years he'd never manned up to the challenge to enter. All he did was to stop around the entrance and do his memorial performance and go home thereafter.

Gossiper slowed down and kept a constant distance of about six yards from his master, and you could tell he was aware of the awfulness of the ghastly place that they now treaded. His fur stood erect along his spine as if he was ready to pounce on a dangerous animal, a snake perhaps. A few paces ahead, and all too suddenly Gossiper stopped and lowered his body and head down, facing the left side of the pathway. He wagged his tail from side to side like a choir master conducting a Christmas carol. Except at that moment, it wasn't in that celebratory mood at all. It was ghostly and frightening. Overhead was a rich greenery of the forest canopy that shielded them from the peering sunlight coming from up above. Archibald stopped, transfixed! He focused his gaze at the direction where possible action was about to ensue. And then he saw it. It was laid there like a strip of an old, dull-colored blanket rotting away on the earth under the grass. It was the biggest snakeskin he'd ever set eyes on. It was like the skin of an anaconda of the Great Amazon River that grew to gigantic lengths untamed.

"Where could the snake be?" he wondered.

He quickly realized that the foul stench could mean one of two things; the snake had just recently molted and perhaps still within the vicinity of the place. The second possibility was more or less the same as the first; the serpent was probably a few yards away from where he stood, burping and dispensing the pungently smelly "antlike" esophageal gases to the surrounding.

Before he could complete his thoughts, it was time for "big bang" action. A giant mega-sized black snake with yellow rings around its neck, approximately two and half meters by his guess with eyelashes like the devil's, shot its head up above the grass with a puffed neck around the throat, as if it was readying its poison glands and prepping to inject a lethal dose into the intruder's flesh. Gossiper was quietly going around it from the other side, and Archibald could only see the shrubs shaking in his trail.

In the blink of an eye, the giant snake dropped its head and slithered fast toward Gossiper like a spear slipping through water. It was fascinating seeing how fast snakes glided in the grass. Within seconds it had caught up with Gossiper, and in a desperate maneuver, Gossiper leapt above the grass, away from it like a frightened deer, but the snake was the master of the game here in the grass arena. It swung around and simultaneously thrashed its head upward toward the dog, and it was surely getting to its target. Its mouth opened wide, fangs exposed, and he could only imagine how this was going to go down. His dog would be dead in minutes with this dangerous snake. He almost couldn't watch the attack. In a moment he remembered how his wife could have been killed, and this couldn't be happening.

"Not again," he declared.

It turned out there were lots of battles going on underneath the vegetation, which Archibald was just beginning to get the full picture of. Right there, barely four meters away, laid an immobilized gray bunny that looked alive, but possibly injured by the snake. They were in a battle for food, and the snake was defending its territory.

Within seconds before striking Gossiper from midair above the short vegetation under the canopy of the forest that hang overhead, Archibald instinctively plucked his arrow from the quiver, his bow already in the left hand and aimed it at the snake's head, trying to be as precise as he could to protect Gossiper at the same time. He was a fast and seasoned archer and could shoot right into the middle of an orange thrown into the sky without missing all day long. To him, hitting the target wasn't a question; it was guaranteed.

For a couple of seconds before he could release the weapon, the snake looked directly into his eyes, as if to say, "I am just defending my catch here," and threw in the towel, dropping its head flat on the ground and slithering away in a bolt. From ten yards away, it popped its head up again as if to say, "This isn't over yet, pal. See you around," and it disappeared into the darkness of the cave never to be seen again. He had a sigh of relief as he called his dog out of the grass.

That was how Gossiper survived. The snake had probably calculated that attacking the dog would've given Archibald just enough time to plant the arrow right inside its head, and the scenario wasn't going to end well, and so it chose life instead. The episode turned out like negotiating a ransom gone awry or like putting a gun on someone's head and having someone else put a gun to your own head. In that situation everyone knows what the best option would be. At least the snake knew that.

The Valley of Death had become part of his story. It was the place where his fiancée had died. Going there had become an annual ritual that Archibald had to perform since her passing. On that fateful day, as he relived the scenes once more, the only remains he had ever found of his wife were blood splatters and a piece of her blouse in the middle of the walk path just a few yards from where the snake attacked them. The piece of her tattered, slimy, and red velvety top had left him with no doubt whatsoever. She was gone and gone for good! And so, he went there to pay homage to the spirit of his beloved Matilda, the love of his life. It was a very important customary practice to him. It connected him to her at the anniversary of her death and made him feel forgiven at least once each year. For far too long he had blamed himself for not being present when she was probably mauled by a wild animal or perhaps swallowed by a nasty, despicable python; who knew? He presumed the responsibility for her death rested at his feet, and he was forever guilty of it.

And for some reason, the coming and the rituals gave him peace and reconciliation with her departed spirit. He now recognized that was part of the reason he never could ever leave and abandon Matanuska region. He had to stay there with her. It was like he was trapped in the place for good. He couldn't betray her. Never. And then again, the feeling was always marred and haunted with the sense of unresolved mystery that he'd never find peace with.

Sometimes he felt like if there were ways of a quick and automated reincarnation for loved ones who'd died under mysterious circumstances to return in the blink of an eye, inform those left behind that they were fine and in a better place, forgive and/or be forgiven as a final means to bring closure, he'd probably be a happy man by now. He would have made peace and probably left this place.

But life had its way settled long before we were here. All he had was to live with it—painfully. He felt helpless and defeated by it. That was his story—a story tied up to his beloved wife-to-be, then to her spirit, and eventually to the land which he now finds himself so much a part of: Susitna River Valley.

Chapter Seven

ANOTHER DAY IN THE CAVE

Just the very next day Archibald was at the same spot with Gossiper, and he walked straight down the same path, along the way did the exact same things he had always done. He stood once or twice, admiring the daffodils at the side of the path, saw a couple of beautifully colored birds fly leisurely by, and followed them intently with his gaze like an ardent ornithologist as they diminished in the distance like tiny specks of sand in the sky. He was a renowned admirer of nature. A cricket hissed nearby and another far off, giving the full meaning of his immersion in the natural environment and nature. The scene was always the same: beautiful and perfect. He continued moving undistracted as he neared his destination.

Once they got to the forest edge, the canopy enveloped them yet again, and soon he and Gossiper were at the same spot as the day before. He saw the gray bunny that the snake had injured during their face-off. It was still laying facedown, but with its long ears stiffened from rigor mortis. Gossiper broke the silence with a bark. And then he continued barking repeatedly as though to signal to Archibald that something was amiss. He kicked the bunny over to check if it was left intact by the snake, or if its belly was split open by the serpent while it preyed on it, ripping off its entrails. He looked around, trying to figure out why Gossiper was barking and jumping up instead of looking at the dead rabbit laying in front of him. Tense and alert, he scanned the environment just to be sure everything was in order and safe.

At this point, he recalled how the snake had behaved the day before, thrusting its head up from approximately ten yards away as if to warn him he'd be back and shuddered. In a swift surprise, he was stunned when the very same snake lashed swiftly right to the neck of Gossiper from up above the tree branch, inserted its yellowish, dirty fangs into the flesh, and bent its neck backward in a momentary jolt, as if to unleash and inject the maximum amount of poison into the dog. That was when he understood why Gossiper was barking and looking up, but it was too late. The damage was inflicted. It was over.

The snake, having done that within seconds, let the dog loose, turned to Archibald, and looked him in the eye as if to say, "I told you so." The dog feebly moaned in a faintly fading growl, tumbled on the dewy grass, and laid in an unmistakable stillness.

"Oh, no! Oh no! This can't be happening to Gossiper!" exclaimed Archibald.

He wondered what he was going to do going forward, but the answers weren't coming. He knew he couldn't live without his best friend, only friend, and companion. Gossiper was dead! "What a tragedy!" he mourned. He was struck with bitterness, rage, and surprise all at once. He tried to reach for his arrow, but this time it was too late for him too. The snake wasn't giving away anything this time. No split second was wasted. It was time for revenge. A fight for supremacy for that forest territory. The snake had quickly uncoiled itself from the tree branch above and elastically reached into the grass below, darted toward Archibald, lashed at him, and in five seconds it had reached its target. Prick!

Again, having summoned more poison from its glands a second time, it had planted its two pairs of dangerously curved fangs into Archibald's neck. The pain that he felt was beyond measure and comprehension. Perhaps it was thirteen out of ten on a scale of one to ten. Putting it in perspective, he felt like red-hot burning coals were poured down his throat. And then there was the blurriness that engulfed him, clouding him like he was drowning into a lukewarm liquid. He saw billows of white smoke that became whiter and whiter like dense fog enveloping him. He felt light-headed like he was swimming in the clouds.

Fighting hard to focus, it was simply impossible no matter how hard he tried. His strength was failing him. He felt powerless and numb. His legs felt faint and weak. He heard Gossiper moaning faintly as he tumbled down on his knees, rolled over, and descended into oblivion and nothingness. For some reason, he felt like his mind was still floating somewhere and thought, *am I dead or dying?* He tried to lift his fingers, but he couldn't. It scared him, and he was afraid soon he'd lose his floating consciousness as well; and he figured, when that happened, he'd probably be dead for real and gone forever. He sprawled out his tongue as though he was a thirsty animal seeking water in a scorched desert. There was a scratch on his chest, then on his face, and he involuntarily jerked. And, finding his strength for the first time after minutes, he lifted his trunk up quickly before he got killed for real. He couldn't believe what was going on. He was alive… It was unbelievable! Even the furry skin that he had rested his head on while he slept had plausibly deceived him as though they were grass blades in the dream.

Still sweating profusely, with his heart rate going through the roof with a hysterical speed of 120 beats every 60 secs, that was a record-breaking nightmare, perhaps the worst yet; and had Gossiper not woken him up, he probably would've died in his sleep. He sat in his papyrus bed for a minute to calm himself down.

"What kind of dream was that which came so alive and so real?" he wondered.

He stroked his dog a little on the neck, got up, scooped some drinking water from his storage pot at the corner, drunk it in sips as if it was hot chai until the calabash was empty, and went back to bed. Luckily, he slept through the rest of the night without any weird dreams. He woke up thinking about it and tried to find any meaning in it if he could. He was disturbed, but grateful it was a dream.

After completing his morning routines, Archibald reached up to the ceiling rafters over the fireplace above the sooty, blackened wire mesh on which he kept and preserved his smoked meat and mushroom. He'd learned the art of fresh-food preservation in this off-the-grid place by relying on salting, sun-drying, and smoking. He discovered, whenever done properly, he could keep his meat for long periods. That was very vital to him as a hunter who always got abundant meat in no time after shooting a few arrows. Taking out a two-pound chunk of dried deer meat, he broke it into smaller pieces and started boiling it in the clay pot over the burning coals.

After a while, he cleaned freshly dug potatoes, chopped red ripe tomatoes, then pepper and onions, and added everything into the mix. He finally left it to simmer in moderately low heat. The beautiful aroma filled the tiny cottage, prompting him to open the door wide to clear and lighten the air density and fogginess of the inside. As he sat waiting for the food to get done, his mind wandered back on the dream of the previous night; and he scrolled through it again in his mind's eye, scanning for any real interpretation that he could get out of it.

As he thought it over and over, his perspective became clearer, and he asked himself the key questions: what if he found himself and Gossiper in the same situation in real life? Would he survive the attack from the giant serpent? He honestly realized that the answer would be no. He and Gossiper would definitely be beaten hands down. The reason was simple; he didn't have the appropriate weaponry for close combat. To be effective and fast enough with an arrow, he needed to be at least four yards away from the target. Once too close, an arrow becomes not the weapon of choice. He needed to fix that. He needed a sword. The short knives he constantly kept in his hunting pouch too were not the right weapons for that kind of scenario.

After his heavy lunch, which looked more like he was celebrating his escape from death in the nightmare, he went behind the cottage down at the porch where he'd kept a pile of broken woods, metal scraps, and tools and dug through it, trying to find something he could mold or forge into a weapon. He finally found an eighteen-inch iron bar from which he began crafting his first real sword purposed for close combat.

Although the metal looked rusted, he was delighted with the find, especially after scraping the outside coating and discovering that it was strong and steely from the core as though it was brand-new. He spent the following three days crafting it in fire and polishing it, and at last, it was precisely shaped as he deemed fit. For some reason, he felt happy and contented with his accomplishment, as though he was a soldier preparing for an impending war. Maybe there was war in the offing, and being a vet, he wasn't scared of war having been engaged in actual combat multitudes of times years ago. Only time would tell what was to come. After resting, he whistled to Gossiper, and off to the woods they went so he would find a good twenty-inch piece of wood that he'd use as a sword simulator to train for close-combat fight. Within an hour they were back, and he was at work shaping his "wooden sword" for training. Settled, he rested for the day.

Chapter Eight

Raising Crops

Hunting used to be his primary occupation while Matilda was solely in charge of the crop husbandry. However, since she passed on, he was forced to learn the hard way the dynamics of how things worked with crops. He soon discovered there was more to the art of cropping than he had initially thought. To him, cropping was a simple and straightforward affair that involved seeding and harvesting without any technical know-how, but the fact that it was a complex operation became crystal clear after Matilda was gone.

Cropping was a hard thing to do, but if he wanted his diet to be complete, including greens, then that was the only way. He did all he could, and with his consistent effort, the small garden was up and running with everything taking shape. He grew carrots, potatoes, lettuce, celery, squash, zucchini, melon, corn, and yams among others. For meat, he didn't have any problem as you already know. Hunting was his best chore, and he loved it.

The springtime of that year was going to be particularly special and an exciting one. The reason being the past winter was so bitter and unforgiving for the most part. In a couple of days, they were going to be in a fully-fledged warm weather. The countryside was glowing with beauty of a well-tendered floral garden. The sweet aromatic smells of nectarines puffed the atmosphere with natural beauty as though it was a free roadside boutique. The birds were happy too, and their beautiful songs evidently more vibrant, as if they were affirming the dawn of the new season with their high-pitched chirping as the ultimate proof. Talking of the birds,

Archibald loved their singing, even though they destroyed his crops especially during the harvest. The red tomatoes were the most affected by the birds, and so he had to build a little scarecrow that helped in case he wasn't around the compound to ward them off.

Activities, chores, and good weather—Archibald loved it all. He enjoyed his walks in the fields, especially when he got to do it aimlessly without any real purpose—just doing for the heck of it. He recalled a day years ago when he had to let a warthog pass by unharmed without arrows flying after it even though he had his bow and arrows ready as he always did. To him, it was truce time, and he was going to respect it. And whenever he was just taking a friendly walk, Gossiper, too, wouldn't attack unless they were both on duty for a real hunting expedition. In case of an attack by unfriendly foes, the truce wouldn't count at least in the name of self-defense. But when all was undisturbed and tranquil, there was peace for all. That was his golden rule. Live and let live.

As the season rolled on, occasionally it rained heavily and sometimes for days nonstop. The sogginess and fogginess that came with the rains presented some of his most bothersome moments, and so he would just resort to cooking his best dishes and confined himself in his tiny abode.

If anything drove Archibald to crop husbandry, look no farther than the making of his favorite drink, the ales. You could call it ginger ale, but because he concocted it with a bunch of other ingredients like lemongrass, lemon, ginger root extracts, sugarcane juice, and food color, he best named it *Locale*. He and Matilda simply coined the term from local and ale, thus *local + ale*. The recipe only required them to mix the ingredients, put the food color of choice, which was normally tea leaves, then boil and leave it to cool off and enjoy.

When they first settled at the Riverside, their main goal was to try to live their life as independently as possible. For that,

Archibald only visited one tiny canteen at the edge of the settlement in Anchorage to buy the basic supplies twice a year. On his bike, he could make the journey within hours, and by evening he'd be back at the cottage where Matilda would be waiting. For sugar, they relied on sugarcane, which they pounded in a mortar to extract the juice.

And so making the drink was good for him for the memory of how they put together the original recipe of their favorite drink. It connected him to the past in a special way. It was his drink for happiness and fond memories.

Sometimes Archibald would walk in the backyard garden, and by doing so, he'd be using nature as an entertainer and soul-soothing therapy. The garden was as attractive as though it was Joseph's biblical coat of many colors. It was spotted with flamboyantly colored daffodils, purplish-ginger plant flowers, among other arrays of spectacular floral varieties that randomly graced the plot. While there, he would walk to each beautiful flower and stand there, occasionally squatting down to examine it more closely, admiring and taking it all in. That was his springtime ritual that he performed seasonally.

As he stood there, the sunniness would be fluctuating in intensity as the clouds would cover and uncover the face of the sun from moment to moment, shifting the temperature dynamics from warm to hot and then to moderate in a beautiful splendor of nature, as though the sun would be playing peekaboo with the earth, using the clouds as hiding blankets. Those were cherished leisure moments for him.

His home-keeping came full circle when he learned how to fend off parasitic ants and bugs by using his improvised primitive and yet effective methods. On soggy days, when tiny ants were most active in food collection, he would spread ashes around the cottage like a chemical perimeter to cordon off the porch from the tiny intruders. The ashes as he learned later contained some chemicals that irritated the ants and deterred them off. They couldn't stand the smells of soda ash or sodium carbonate that was part of its chemical composition.

For the flying bugs, he sprayed a portion of his concentrated lemongrass extracts that exuded some pyrethrum-like smells, acting as a chemical repellent to especially mosquitoes. Matilda used to do all those things, but now he had to perform the tasks himself. That made him appreciate her posthumously even more, having practically seen and delved into the magnitude of what she used to go through and accomplish on their behalf. In his cropping, the challenge that he faced the most was the storage of his harvests.

He therefore preferred to keep the potatoes underground in the garden for as long as he could before digging them out. For the tomatoes, he started eating them as soon as they were mature even when still green. Fresh from the garden to his cooking pot was the way he liked it.

Chapter Nine

A Sign on the Roof

Working on the little garden had become a trivial pastime activity for him if he wasn't out in the woods hunting. One day, while Archibald was busy harvesting some potatoes and carrots for his next day's cooking, he lifted his face from his work, looked up toward the house, and there it was, a tiny little fellow. A beautifully colored little bird—the harbinger of peace as the robin was known in the area. It was perched there at the pinnacle of the cottage, looking the other way.

As soon as Archibald looked at it, although the robin was facing the other direction, with its little legs, it jumped around and faced him as if to acknowledge that he saw him. With its red chest, he knew it was a male. The robin opened its tiny wings as if to embrace Archibald from a distance and bowed like a Frenchman tipping his hat to a comrade. Archibald raised his hand slowly and waved gently, being cautious not to scare his little guest away. He looked intently at it as it started its majestic performance of singing, chirping continuously, minute after minute as he continued with his harvesting and occasionally turning his face, as if to say, "go on, I see you."

He thought of all the crazy superstitions that he'd heard about this little creature. Some said it was symbolic of new beginnings when you dreamed of this bird. Others said if a robin flew into your house, you'd become rich, and many encounters with the robin symbolized even greater wealth. But this time the robin was just performing to him on the roof. He thought of how seamen used bird signs to interpret conditions and assessed good and bad luck as they sailed in the high seas. Albatrosses circling around the ship for example was said to indicate good weather, but a robin singing on the roof, *What could it be? A sign from the other world perhaps.* He looked up at it again and tried to figure out its message… if any.

He thought of the message poetically, supposedly to harness a divine revelation or a discernment if that was even possible. He wasn't so much like looking forward to any good luck, but if it would be anything that would prevent a thing like losing a family member, he was all for it. For now, his only family was Gossiper, and he couldn't even bring himself to think of anything that would hurt him. The devastation would be existential for him. He would probably give up life and die there in that land. But that wasn't to be planned. If ever he'd end up there, he'd be grateful after all so he could finally join Matilda in the afterlife. That was the only reason he'd love to finally breathe his last in that mountain slope.

Besides that, joining society and living a normal life again was a distant possibility that lingered on his mind from time to time. The only thing he lacked was concrete motivation. There was nothing to compel him or drive him to do it. So far, it was naught. Zero. He couldn't think of it. His thought dashed back again on the robin, and he ran the poem through his mind:

> *Little fellow, my tiny guest, what say you of that which lay ahead into tomorrow?*
>
> *Is it but a beautiful event or encounter that awaits me, little fellow?*
>
> *I think I can smell a sweet aroma close to me, little fellow.*
>
> *Perhaps I should say thank you little fellow for your service and good tidings.*
>
> *In the song that you sing, I see vitality and bliss.*
>
> *You shoot straight into the sky as if to grab luck from the heavens and place it upon my cottage, little fellow, is that true?*
>
> *Thank you, little fellow, and as you fly off, know ye that I am happy and in anticipation of a beautiful tomorrow.*
>
> *Glad tidings, little fellow.*

As he finished his mental poetry, he shrugged it off even though the robin continued with its performance endlessly until he was done. When he rose up to collect the harvest, the robin flew straight up into the air one last time, then back on the cottage, and finally flew away toward a nearby *jacaranda* bush.

The trees looked like jacaranda, and so he simply called it the jacaranda bush. One more chore, and he'd take his break. He took his wooden wheelbarrow, loaded the twenty-gallon capacity container, and headed toward the river. Down at the river, he drew a full container of water and headed back, pulling the wheelbarrow backward that made it a lot easier. He made sure collecting water was an easy job in his isolated home by ensuring the ball bearings of the wheels were always generously lubricated.

With enough water collected for the day, he laid down on his papyrus mat and took a siesta. Gossiper laid across the room from him, tongue popped out as he panted the heat and fatigue of the day away.

As the evening overcame the heat of the sun, the horizon zeroed down on it, prepared to blanket it off from his side of the world. Black clouds hung over the dark-green vegetation far in the skyline, dimming the light of the setting sun even more. The hot orange sky dulled off into a light-maroon coloration as the sun finally kissed goodbye. The mountain shadows towered over the land, enveloping everything. And then it was the beginning of the night.

The crescent moon suddenly appeared from the opposite direction as if it was an opposition leader conflicting with the sun and trying to fill the void left. As the sun's light disappeared off the loop, the moon steadily assured the earth dwellers that there was hope. Soon it was bright just enough. A fox hollowed in the distance as if to grace the night, and thereafter followed by another further away. It was as though they were flirting through an open communication network of the jungle. Perhaps the first one was a male, asking the second hollower out to which the assumed answer was yes. The hollowing continued, and soon it got a little chaotic. Multitudes of bugs, crickets, plus other nocturnal animals all joined in their nightly choruses, and nature assumed full control.

Archibald hadn't realized how fatigued he'd been perhaps until he placed his form down on the mat. By the time he woke up, he'd slept through the evening, and it was bedtime, this time for real.

He took a quick bath and got back in bed for the night. Gossiper always had a choice either to sleep out in the porch or indoors. He had his way of deciding that, and all Archibald did was leave the door in such a way he could get in and out as he pleased.

For a tired man, the night was always short. Archibald was wavering between sleep and wakefulness. But the incessant songs of the early rising birds made his sleep even sweeter. The chirping soothed him like the morning drizzle in the winter. He was dreamy in generalities, but with no specifics on anything, just cozily floating there in dreamland. He finally found himself awake to his dismay.

He had his plans set for the day, and he was going to prepare himself a lofty meal. Much of the recipe was intact and ready, but part of it remained at large. He needed some fish to get the soup going. And so, after the cleanups, he and Gossiper dashed off to Little Susitna River for a catch. They headed to the side where the chum salmon, and silver salmon were predominant. He hoped to catch one of those salmons, or if he was lucky, the humpback white fish wouldn't be bad at all. He was like a hunter who didn't have to choose, and so he was open to whatever would nibble at his fishing hook. Within minutes they were down to business and luck was on their side. He was able to catch seven salmons and two humpback white fish within just twenty-five minutes. Each was weighing not less than 3.5 pounds, with the biggest approximately 5 pounds.

He struggled with his heavy load back home, and once he'd rested, he started the cleaning process to get the meal ready. Was that the luck his little guest, the robin, spoke and performed about yesterday on the roof? Was that the whole message he really needed to know that badly, or the streak of luck was just beginning? Well, catching those many fish in just under thirty minutes had never happened to him before, but still it wasn't that phenomenal to qualify as a message from the gods. He yearned for more evidence to justify his superstitious beliefs, but there seemed none that was convincing thus far.

Chapter Ten

A Brush with the Violent Side of Nature

Historically, Alaska had been one of the quietest states when it came to tornadoes and earthquakes. Being the largest state in America with vast mountainous plains on its outline, Alaska was and continues to be a mystery to many. Endowed with fantastic topography with an array of animal species and birds that attracted ornithologists from across the nation and the globe were some of the attributes that came to mind when you thought of Alaska. It was simply an adventurer's paradise.

Unlike Oklahoma and Texas, placed along the tornado alley that received lion's share of twisters yearly, Alaska was far off like a silent spectator state with almost none. Even though the history had been graceful and smooth for decades, the status quo got shattered that peaceful year, which had started with normalcy. It started quietly like an ordinary day, and Archibald was inside the cottage, taking a catnap on the mat. Outside it was cloudy with cumulus piling up upon each other in the sky like an artist's tie and dye design. Soon afterward the stained cotton clouds blackened into low-altitude nimbus, pregnant and ready to shower the earth below.

It wasn't exclusively a rainy day, but there was just a threatening chance of a light drizzle, although with an unrealistically strong accompanying wind.

Down on the mat, Archibald felt the vibration and the thundering, got up, and dashed outside to make up what was happening. He looked in the distance, and what he saw befuddled him. There was a light drizzle, mixed with tiny hails, some half inch in diameter falling from the sky. It was getting intense by the minute. That wasn't the only major astonishment he saw brewing. The dark clouds were worryingly flying lower and lower and losing altitude progressively as they headed to his direction.

"Come on, man. This is Alaska, for heaven's sake," Archibald blurted the words involuntarily. "This is a silent zone, remember," he continued as though he was speaking to reprimand nature directly.

As the dark, now whitish, clouds rushed toward the tiny cottage from about a mile away, Archibald started his safety protocol and wanted to run back in and lay down in the tiny, hollow corner of the room, but he was not settled to do that without getting Gossiper indoors first. He whistled to him, but he wasn't anywhere in sight. By then the wind speed was a tantalizing seventy miles per hour. He was almost getting swept off his feet. He tightly held onto a pole by the door, his vision almost blinded by the flying debris and dust.

The nimbus clouds that were miles away minutes ago were now probably less than a mile, spiraling and twirling like the trail of a downed jet engine. Shockingly, it was getting extremely low, as though the heaven was reaching down to kiss the earth. Three hundred yards, and his fears were confirmed! The kiss became reality. And that wasn't for good. He had a fully blown twister, and suddenly his tiny little living quarter had become an epicenter of a devastating wrath of nature.

Within minutes the quiet mountainous countryside was covered in debris and dust like a barren landscape on the Red Planet. The only contrast was the rich greenery that enveloped this place and the icy mountaintops unlike the barrenness that characterized the surface of planet Mars. It was crazy.

He continued to hold onto the supporting pole at the door side, poked his head outside, and whistled again and again to Gossiper, but this time he wasn't responding. He looked up toward the tip of the twister that reached into the sky beyond the low-altitude clouds.

"Whoa, whoa, whoa!"

Up in the middle of the swirling dust, mixed with the clouds approximately twenty-five yards above the ground, he saw in disbelief! Right there in the middle of it was Gossiper, picked up and was struggling and spiraling like a piece of carrot going down the toilet. The twister headed away, taking Gossiper with it. Archibald was torn between two hard choices. Either to let go of the pole and try to run and follow the twister that was spiraling away with his one and only friend or stay put, save his own life, and let fate take its course.

He chose the first option; he'd rather die trying to save his friend, the only family he had, than stick to the pole like a coward and be left to live alone in this island with nobody else. He left and darted toward the hurricane, whistling to Gossiper, trying not to give up. He scuttled along peripherally as the twister made its way toward the jacaranda bush where the robin had flown the other day. In a lucky twist, Gossiper's weight played to his advantage, and he was lowered just above the tallest tree of the bush. He was slammed on the top branch, tangled up and damped in the wake of the storm. He started falling as the twister edged off to another direction.

Then the impact. Gossiper thudded on the green canopy, driven by gravity, slipping, and hastily headed to the ground. Within seconds he would hit the ground and crush to death. Wait for it; the countdown began in five, four, three, two, and wham! He was stuck just five yards above the ground! As fate would have it, a twined web of creeping shrubs and branches held him up like a nature-woven hammock from God himself. With the twister on its way away, Archibald hurried to Gossiper and yanked him down toward himself.

He held him and fell gently down with him to the ground, stroked his neck, sobbing and repeatedly saying, "You are all right, pal. You made it, you made it!"

That was like a nasty swipe by a violent twister that almost swept away his entire livelihood. He looked at Gossiper again, checked his legs, neck, ribs, and head just to make sure he didn't break any bones.

Amazingly, everything was fine, and he walked him back to the cottage, still recovering from the shock. It was a brush with the hostile side of nature. He was relieved they were both alive and well.

Chapter Eleven

BACK TO THE BEGINNING

With all settled in the aftermath of the twister, Archibald held his head in his hands so he could think clearly about the whole thing. He ran his thoughts down to the day he met Matilda at Hotel Anchorage in downtown Anchorage City, Alaska, where he worked as a security guard… Back then he was living as a civilized gentleman, what he called normal life within a community. It was simple, straightforward life full of regular expectations and predictable outcomes. He stretched his thoughts farther back then to the days when he was in active military service and how he fought his way back from the battle fields into society and started off as a young vet. He was scanning through history and trying to put his life into perspective so he could identify where things started going off track. And then he saw the connection.

It was clear that in his previous life, food and services were available whenever he had the cash to purchase. It was a cash economy 2.0. Ordinary and simplistic life. And then how funny it all changed. It was with Matilda that the shift all started. After their first encounter, she wanted their second date to be unique, and so they planned a picnic in the countryside. They purchased a huge tent and large quantities of supplies. Perhaps the mistake he made was to pack fishing hooks and an arrow set with a bow. The picnic turned out phenomenal, and he reminisced it with a smile on his face as he closed his eyes to relive the beautiful experience once more.

They had had the best time of their entire life together in the jungle. For five days they ate purely organic foods prepared from scratch. He recalled the tranquility and the serenity that the solitary life provided. From it all, they learned one thing: the peace derived from the silence and quietness was simply priceless, and no city in the world could provide that. It was like surrendering up to nature and enabling one's soul to partake of natural beauty that was soothingly extraordinary: the bird songs, the open starry sky of the night, and the bright-yellow sunset at dusk were so real and breathtaking; things that city dwellers barely noticed in their busy, rat-race lives. To discover the peace of nature was surely a privilege. That was what they both agreed on.

They passed time at the river on some days and would just sit at the side to listen to the water flapping the waves on the banks incessantly for hours. The fish of the little Susitna River would be putting up their splash shows, popping up to the surface occasionally to catch some air above the water, and it was utterly incredible. The kingfishers also did their stylistic aerial spearfishing, adding more fun to the menu of sights to be seen at the shores. It was awesome. The fishy and the algal smells of the river, coupled with the lushness of the soggy environment, were too authentic to be forged. To two town dwellers that they were, that was an experience of a lifetime.

When they depleted their food supplies, Archibald proposed they could try to gather some things locally and stay for two more days before returning to his rented apartment in the town, since Matilda's booking at the Anchorage Hotel was already over. With his bow and arrow, Archibald shot a deer, and that was worth meat for seven days! During the brief hunt, Matilda herself caught two huge silver salmons that same day, and in just a short moment, the food shortage was averted. They had three pounds of rice left, and with that, they stayed for three weeks straight. They soon discovered they could just grow potatoes, and that could take them for as long as they wanted.

On the day they finally agreed to go back home, which wasn't easy, Matilda was packing their luggage when Archibald dropped to his knee and popped the question.

"Will you do me the honors to be my wife?"

There was a long silence, followed by a "yes" with an explanation. "I want to marry you, but my yes isn't for immediately. I hope you'll understand that we can do it at a better time in the future rather than now."

Archibald thought long and said, "At least that's better than a 'no.' So, can I say we're officially betrothed to each other from now onwards, is that correct?"

"That's absolutely correct, sir," Matilda responded.

"Matilda, I want you to know that I did that because of the situation at hand. You're a foreign national and would be returning to Europe in a couple of days, and so I thought you'd get past the fact that we haven't dated for any reasonably long time yet to warrant this rather unexpected proposal from me. I just thought I should get that out of my chest," he concluded.

"I understand," she replied.

For days they tried to readjust back to their normal life, but the noise wasn't making it any easier. It was exhausting and annoying, especially because they were powerless to do anything about it. It was what it was.

On the third day, Archibald asked Matilda, "Are you thinking what I am thinking?"

"Yes! We're going back, aren't we?"

"That's what I am talking about," Archibald replied.

With the last bit of money they had, they purchased the

relevant materials to make a cottage, especially the roof and other basic supplies. It was going to be a prolonged picnic this time. The rest you already know. Whenever they needed cash for supplies, Archibald had maintained contact with some town dwellers to whom he could simply supply fresh fish and game meat for cash. They mostly needed soap, oil, salt, plus other basic needs. Their life was the best.

It was good generally, except that it was tragically cut short when Matilda was killed under mysterious circumstances. He didn't find her body for proper burial, though. He just found patches of blood and a piece of her cloth. He looked for days before he drew the conclusion that she must have died. The blood and shreds of her blouse evidence left no doubt to him. It became so hard to report the incident back in the town, fearing he'd be held liable to her disappearance, especially because her body wasn't found. After a while, he had to make it a tightly guarded secret. For his protection, he decided he'd state to the authorities he was still looking for her if apprehended and accused of foul play in her disappearance or possible homicide.

Even though he'd pledged to live there forever, the tornado that just ravaged his abode almost made him change his mind. It frightened him to the core. And for a moment, he doubted if he could continue to live in solitude there. He wondered if he could return to the ordinary predictable life and to the people. It was a tough and confusing moment.

But on the flip side, he was by then so used to the thrill of nature, the unpredictability there, the jungle and the natural surroundings. For example, whenever he would set out to go hunting, he wouldn't know exactly what would end up in his plate for dinner. He would later feast on whatever would be his catch for the day. No bills to worry about. No payment. No loans. Everything was organic, fresh, and sweet. All he did was renewed his fishing and hunting licenses annually. The fruit of the land and the river were there in abundance.

In his abode he rested better and did everything pretty much in his own terms, his own schedule and time. He didn't have a watch, but if he had one, he would've probably thrown it away already. He didn't need it. In his new place he'd turned the rules upside down. Time was under his control. He was never late for anything, always on time. He loved it, but for the tornado, it was a different story. It nearly picked up the entire cottage from its base, just missing by barely twenty yards.

And so, he asked himself the question, "What if it happened again?"

That was a question without a definite answer. It was a nagging one that never went away for days.

Chapter Twelve

THE BIRTHDAY VACATION

Turning twenty-one was like a milestone that took too long to achieve to a teenager feeling the brunt of parental control, especially in a family built on strong religious foundation. All three of Matilda's closest friends, Mia Joseph, aged twenty, Lucija, nineteen, and Iva, twenty, all declared they couldn't wait to turn twenty-one so they could get on with their lives as independent adults.

In the mid-1950s Yugoslavia was rife with religiosity, and the practice was growing even stronger year after year due to the then— newly revitalized leadership and political stability. Andreas Juergen, Matilda Juergen's father, grew up in the post-Nazi Germany where he was born and raised. He was part of the elitist population that was a prominent driving force responsible for the brewing German economic miracle of the 1950s, the then-popular *Wirtschaftswunder* that saw the Federal Republic of West Germany after World War II surge economically to become one of the most prosperous nations in the whole of Europe. On the other hand, her mother was raised in the popular culture of former Yugoslavian conservatism, with strong communist influence where raising children under strict religious codes and keeping them on straight societal lines was part of the norms.

Catholicism had deep roots from the mid eighteenth century; although there was a mix of Orthodox church from the early 1920s, which was a strong signature of Russian influence. As the Catholic church grew in prominence, the Orthodoxy practice declined, but the tradition was fully established. Instilling discipline in children was therefore a good part of the culture, except that the kids always looked at it differently. Turning twenty-one, therefore, was quite a huge deal. Matilda was ready, and her demeanor clearly exuded that crystalline resolve to embrace the next chapter of her life on her own.

When it clocked midnight on June 24, that year of our Lord 1951, she couldn't hide her smile in the shadow of darkness within the confines of her room, knowing that she was finally free to sail solo in almost anything she wanted to do in her life. She could officially get a boyfriend, get married, take a trip abroad, and go far away from Europe entirely, miles away from her parents for the first time like a free bird. She almost screamed and only had to muffle the sound with her pillow, "Hurray! I am twenty-one!" She felt like bursting into a song and screaming to the top of her lungs and waking the entire neighborhood with the good news. But she had to exercise self-control like an adult then going forward, so she calmed herself down and laid her head back on the pillow.

As she slept for the remaining part of the night, she dreamed she was sailing in the vast Pacific with her high school pals in a yacht, merrymaking. As she recalled, she was enjoying every bit of it, grooving in the rave with her peers like a bunch of athletes training for the Olympics. The visuals, the audios, and the waves slapping the keel and the side of the yacht all came alive and so legit she thought it was real, only to be disappointed after waking up to realize it was all a myth happening in dreamland.

"That was really nice," she whispered to the pillow and wished it wasn't just a smoky dream.

Nonetheless, the euphoria of the occasion still graced the atmosphere, and she felt like she was a different version of herself. A more vibrant and energetic Matilda she'd become. She woke up smiling and went on to make breakfast, which was customary on her birthdays. She always celebrated with three meals starting off with a bunch of her close friends who lived within the vicinity of the neighborhood coming around for the first meal of the day—breakfast. All her closest friends did the same, and they all made effort to attend each other's all three parties of their birthdays.

The living room was packed with guests. All of a sudden, they burst into a song: Sretan rođendan ti

Sretan rođendan ti

Sretan rođendan, sretan rođendan

Sretan rođendan ti

Još jedna svjećica za zapaliti

Na tvojoj rođendanskoj torti

Neka ti se sve želje ostvare

Sada idemo slaviti

The English version would probably be preferred by many as opposed to the Croatian one above:

"Happy birthday to you, happy birthday to you, happy birthday… dear Matilda-a-a-a, Happy birthday to you"

As the song rang in her parents' living room, Matilda couldn't hold back her tears. It was a momentous occasion. She was officially twenty-one and an adult. She was ready to flap her wings and look outside of her parents' home into the unknown. It was a scary and liberating feeling all at the same time.

After she blew the candles and made a wish, it was gift time. She opened a huge box from one of her most favorite pals, Mia Joseph; she'd bought for her a beautiful party outfit that took her breath away.

"Thank you so much, honey," she labored emotionally with

the words, reached out and hugged Mia tightly, and whispered softly into her ears, "You're the best." She opened the rest of the packages, a total of thirteen boxes. One of them, from her parents, contained an envelope with a card on which the following words were inscribed:

You are the love of our lives, Matilda. The perfect gift from above, and we'd never trade you for anything in this world. Thank you for being a part of our family. We have to honestly say that your twenty-first birthday is a bittersweet ceremony for us. On the one side we're so thrilled you've grown into a beautiful and intelligent lady, and on the other side we feel anxious and scared that we'll see less and less of you as you continue to build your life and chart the course of your future. Maybe it is what all parents go through no matter what. A time for the chicks to leave the nest. We saw it coming…and here we are.

However dreadful it might seem, we're still so proud of who you've become and wish you the very best as you start this new chapter of your life. Our humble gift to you is a fully funded trip to any place of your choice on the planet to vacate for two weeks.

Please let us know your chosen destination, and we'll help you with the travel arrangements and booking.

With much love from Mr. and Mrs. Juergen

As she read the card, the room fell dead silent, and you could hear a pin drop on the tiled floor. It was like the world had stood still and motionless, with only her tears rolling down her cheeks. She put the card on the table and threw herself on both her parents in total surrender to their love overflowing. Kneeling between them, she cried a cry of submission and love. It felt as though this was a goodbye moment, and yet to her it was just another birthday; although the way she was being treated this time was making it special, and she could acknowledge that too.

The following day Matilda had her destination chosen; she was vacationing in the United States of America. Specifically, she was heading to the mountainous Territory of Alaska in Anchorage City, via New York. She was eager to escape for a moment from the liberal Yugoslavian territory, which was still learning and getting used to living in freedom and independence that was being asserted by the then—prime minister, Josip Broz Tito, who was politically leaning away from the Soviet Union's totalitarian influence. She wanted to taste the so-called American freedom firsthand even if for only two weeks. Seeing it in the movies and reading about it from the pages of books weren't enough any longer.

With her parents' help, they booked tickets and traveled with her to Frankfurt, Germany, by train and spent one night together before her flight from Frankfurt International Airport the following day. Her father, Mr. Andreas Juergen, had his family there, and they were paying them a visit after almost three years of not hearing much from them. The cousins and the friends that she'd always spent holidays with had almost all grown up themselves. It was a beautiful reunion; nonetheless, she had to cut it short the next day as she headed to America. She planned to stop by after her vacation and stay for at least a week before returning to Zagreb by rail. Everything was so exciting.

Matilda expected the original Convair CV-240, the American breed of planes that were designed to replace the old ubiquitous Douglas DC-3 to take her to America. They were a newer, sleeker version with pressurized cabins and definitely more comfortable. She was flying for the first time, of course, thanks to her loving, generous parents for sacrificing part of their savings to usher her into adulthood in style.

The itinerary ran from Frankfurt to New York City and then to Anchorage City, Alaska. Soon after takeoff, Matilda immersed herself in a play, Death of a Salesman, written by the American playwright, Arthur Miller, in 1949, which had won him the Pulitzer

Prize for drama the same year. She was sharpening her English, which was quite good already, save for a little work she needed to polish her accent. She was a prolific reader, and for the trip she'd had more reason to pick up a couple more books for her reading before she left. She delved into the plot in the book, reading about *Willy Loman, the fictional character who was the salesman in the story...*

The flight was smooth for most of the journey over the Atlantic Ocean, save for a little turbulence that they experienced briefly two hours into the flight. She looked out the window occasionally, and it was beautiful seeing a white chunk of snow spread over the vast landscape as they flew over what she was later told was Greenland. It was so spectacular. Except the name of the country didn't make much sense to her. If it was up to her, she would've probably named it Snow Land or Whiteland for that matter. She never saw any green down there to justify the name. Well, that was just a piece of her mind. She later learned that when Erik the Red found Greenland, he named it so in order to attract more people to settle there.

They flew on, and in a little over eight hours they landed in New York International Airport, which was opened just a couple of years earlier, and later in 1963 renamed JFK International Airport as a tribute to the thirty-fifth president of the United States after his assassination. After clearing from Customs and Immigration, she waited for another two hours and boarded her connecting flight to Anchorage City, Alaska. A smooth takeoff and a short flight this time. They landed at the Anchorage International Airport at 6:00 p.m., and she got a taxi to Anchorage Hotel where she was booked. Elegance and class were the words to describe the historic hotel. It was originally built in 1916 and revamped in 1936. She was reserved in the far corner in one of the twenty-six luxuriously furnished rooms at the time.

After a hot, relaxing shower, she walked down to the reception and was ushered into the dining area for dinner. She treated herself to a glorious, happy birthday meal for herself and went back to her room to rest from jet lag. She tried to sleep, but it wasn't easy falling asleep. As she thought of what to do, she walked back to the reception and asked the bartender for Stagnum rosé, a popular Yugoslavian wine of the time. The bartender offered her a seat at the corner and asked her to wait. After five minutes, a security guard walked in and headed to the bartender at the counter. They talked for a minute before he came down to Matilda's table. They exchanged greetings, and Matilda gave him a five-dollar bill, which he took and disappeared out into the streets. Fifteen minutes later he reemerged with a bottle of Stagnum rosé, a sparkling red wine in his hand.

Athletic and tall, the guard brought her a glass and handed her the change, but she told him to keep it.

"By the way, I am Archibald," he introduced himself.

She told him her name and thanked him for his courtesy and for the trouble of letting him walk down the streets to a nearby liquor store to get her brand of wine. He thanked her for the change, said good night, and left. Matilda strolled down to her room, drank a glass, and slept like a baby till morning.

She woke up rested but still felt the nagging torture of jetlag, which she was trying hard to rebuff since she landed. After a thorough preparation that included some twenty minutes in the bathtub, application of a simple makeup, she was ready for the morning in the beautiful country. The makeup completed a touch of elegance to match with her beautiful surrounding. Mia Joseph had taught her a thing or two about beauty, and she now realized how vital that lesson was. She wasn't exactly the judge of her looks; the occupants of Anchorage Hotel were. As she walked down, she could feel how she was being noticed and silently approved by the men and the female staffers at the hotel. The guests had the same reaction, and it made her smile even more authentic and natural. Being noticed was a thing that any lady could use, and she was delighted to be at the center of it all. She felt like a newly born celebrity, and she was loving it.

She wore a silvery-green outfit that ran down to her feet like a princess's gown. In a well-calculated pace she strode down to the lobby and headed to the dining hall to join the other guests already settled and digging into their breakfast. The forks, the glasses, and the cups clanked, and the aroma was as welcoming as the staffers themselves. Before she could begin to look confused, a female staff intercepted her at the door and asked if she preferred a particular spot in the hall to which she pointed to the left side. She settled at a table all by herself and started with lemonade then shrimp, fried chicken, scrambled eggs, and a concoction of fruits.

Halfway through her breakfast she saw him; he had a ponytail tied with a ribbon, dressed in the hotel uniform fitting firmly on him as though he was a cowboy except without a gun. She waved, flashing that authentic smile. Archibald smiled back and walked to the table to formally say "hello."

They talked a little, and she said, "I still have the wine by the way, but in case the bottle runs dry, expect a call, that's if you wouldn't mind."

"Not at all, miss. I am available and would love to be of help. Just let me know."

He said bye and left to go do an errand outside.

Chapter Thirteen

A Private Dinner

On day four of her visit, Matilda started her quest to explore the mid-downtown Anchorage City, and she chose not to bother anyone to help her do it. She was going it alone. She was used to cities and needed no help getting around. After breakfast, she informed the receptionist at the front desk, handed her the room key, and walked out through the front door into the streets. The streets were sparsely busy, not too crowded with vehicles, and she only needed to pay attention to the pedestrians walking toward the opposite direction past her. She recited her traveling rule in her thoughts: always guard against thieves in a new environment because you never know what the local culture is and how the people did things.

She felt nice stretching out, having been within the confines of the hotel for almost four days never stepping out. She didn't care about getting lost by any chance, knowing by mentioning the name of the hotel to any of the town dwellers, she'd amply be given direction back. Across the street she saw something that got her thinking, B & B Liquor Store, and thought it was perhaps the place where the gentleman, now her friend, had come for the bottle of wine three nights ago. Archibald—such a kind and handsome man he was. She shook off the thought of him from her mind and entered a printing shop that sold stationery as a side business. Two men, all white, and an African American lady stood on a short queue, and she joined at the tail of the line. She waited for like fifteen minutes and, when it was her turn, asked whether they sold books; and they did, but she wasn't buying any. She was just window-shopping. After checking a few books, she came out and turned around, heading back to the hotel, making it look like she had come to the printing business.

She walked leisurely besides the many cars that lined the sidewalk in a perfectly motionless queue probably parked by workers and the city's businesspeople. Far in the distance she could see the mountain ranges lining up the horizon and wondered what it would be like venturing over there.

"Was it even possible?" she whispered the question to herself as she continued trekking on.

Returning to her room, it was almost lunchtime. Barely quarter of an hour to noon, and she decided to just lay down and take a little nap in a bid to try to shake off the nagging sleep that was still reminding her of Central European Summer Time Zone in Zagreb, Yugoslavia. Luckily for her, it turned out to be a long and deep siesta, and by the time she woke up, it was 7:46 a.m. in the morning back home in Zagreb but 9:46 p.m. in Alaska, United States! Her body was still in perfect sync with her home country, forgetting everything in this foreign land. She felt good and more at ease. She needed the rest after all.

She washed her sleepy face, refreshed quickly, and strolled down to the reception to inquire about the food situation.

Before she could say a word, the lead receptionist was like, "Oh my, miss! Where in heaven have you been the whole time? We didn't see you for lunch and dinner and have been wondering without a clue where the heck you'd disappeared to."

Matilda just smiled and said, "It's the time zone, guys. Jet lag was hammering me big-time. Still is, I am afraid. I guess my system is still lined up with the CEST zone, which unfortunately means right now is my morning, so I better ask for 'breakfast.'" She smiled again. "I just laid down to nap before lunch and woke up almost nine hours later. And right now, I am super hungry, so before I look for any plan B, is there any luck for poor me regarding dinner?"

"Absolutely," Rosette responded. "Just give us twenty-five to thirty minutes and consider the issue properly handled." The countdown started pronto.

"Before you go, since the dining hall is almost cleared, you have the privilege to choose wherever you'd prefer to have your meal from, Miss."

"Can that be in my room?", Matilda asked politely.

"You got it," Rosette responded.

Matilda walked back in and took a quick shower as she prepared to dine. In ten minutes, she was done and out of the shower. She dressed up casually and relaxed with her book. She was down to the last few pages of *Death of a Salesman*. At exactly 10:27 p.m. there was a knock on the door. Rosette walked in with two other staffers, and they set up the table in front of her room chair. They laid an oblong-shaped tray on the table, set a plate of fried chicken, bacon-wrapped scallops with maple syrup that would be the appetizer for her lone feast, baked potato and steak, fully done, fruit mix, dessert of chocolate and whipped cream, and juice.

"Wow! This is unbelievable, guys," Matilda broke the silence as the ladies worked at her table quietly. "This is a lot of food. Well, now I got to say I wish I had a glass of my kind of wine, and that would be the final piece in a complex puzzle, I guess.

As Rosette was delicately moving silverware and glasses on the dinner table, she glanced at Matilda and said, "We thought you'd say that."

As soon as she uttered the words, there was a knock on the door again, Helena, one of the two ladies, reached out and opened.

Archibald entered, one hand holding a mini-chocolate cake with three candles planted on it and a bottle of Rosa Stagnum wine in the other.

As soon as he entered, they burst into a song, "Happy birthday to you, happy birthday to you…" They sang to her, and she was surprised and shocked at the same time.

"Who told you it is my birthday week, guys? I am speechless," Matilda asked.

"Someone called us from your home country," Rosette replied jokingly. "Well, we know a little birdie who whispered to us your secret. Anyway, it was your passport at the guest registry, dear. And then for the wine, the hotel will take care of that too, a little bit of hospitality from us so you can come back again next time or tell someone else to vacation here as well. And, not to forget an important detail, it was him who recommended the brand. So blame him," Rosette said it, pointing at Archibald as they left the room, leaving him to open the bottle.

As soon as they were all out, Matilda quickly rose up, opened her arms to hug him, but asked if he minded before hugging him. You guessed right—he didn't mind at all.

She whispered softly in his ear, "Thank you!" and let go and sat down to eat.

She thanked him again before he could leave and asked how she could reward him for his generosity and help with a little token.

"A dinner perhaps, if you don't mind, in a private place elsewhere, another restaurant."

"That'd be very kind of you, miss, and when were you thinking of that?" Archibald asked eagerly.

"Tomorrow, lunch or dinner, your choice," she responded.

"Well, dinner is okay. I know a place. Not far, not near. Just perfect," Archibald replied.

"Tomorrow then, and thank you."

Archibald walked out, gleaming with smiles, and back to the reception area, ready to clock out for the evening.

At 4:15 p.m. the next day a stocky and heavily set gentleman walked through the front door of Anchorage Hotel and spoke to the receptionist at the front desk. She picked up the telephone receiver and dialed number 24 that corresponded to the room number and spoke inside the mouthpiece before placing it back down. Within a minute Matilda walked into the reception, emerging from the backside. She spoke to Rosette who introduced her to the man standing by. He extended his hand, and they spoke a little before he led her out through the front door into a taxi that was parked nearby in the parking lot. The driver ushered her into the back comfy seat, where she joined a man who was waiting. That man was Archibald, her new friend and date for the night.

They drove off, and within five minutes arrived at their destination. They entered a restaurant and sat in a corner seat. A staffer walked to their table, and they placed their orders, starting with a glass of water for Matilda and a glass of lemonade for Archibald. Matilda then went for chips and salsa for her appetizer, and Archibald asked for a bowl of sour mushroom soup as his start-up. For the main course they went uniform: grilled salmon, baked potatoes with cheese, stuffed green-and-red pepper and baked, and then chicken salads, dessert, and coffee at the end of the meal. They spoke about European cultures and the American ones, travel, wars; and Archibald, being a veteran, was very impressed that Matilda was such a well-rounded conversationalist.

As things winded down, Archibald gathered his courage and asked if they could do it again before she returned to Europe.

"Well, on one condition," she responded.

"And what's that going to be, beautiful lady?" Archibald asked.

"That it would be in a quiet place, in the countryside—someplace serene. Perhaps in the shadows of the mountains," she specified.

They skipped the following day for Archibald to figure out the right spot for what they were now referring to as a picnic. He made a checklist and a "to-do" list and did some asking around, running through the list and checking off each requirement or item to be done in the preparation process. While he preoccupied himself with the preps, Matilda was reminiscing every minute of the last four days and recounting every activity and experience. She was baffled by the receptive American culture and how she'd so quickly made friends with the people and how the interactions had been so easy and welcoming; plus, now she had to contend with the likely possibility of getting an American boyfriend just the next day. Things were pacing up too fast and slipping out of her hands.

But she didn't need to worry, perhaps since she felt safe with the guy, but she still wanted to act with caution and reservation. The only problem was time. She had just a few days, perhaps a week, before returning to Yugoslavia, and she wanted to make the most of the opportunity.

In her own assessment, she'd already fallen in love with the country; and at the back of her mind, she was slipping down into the valley of love with her American pal, but the only scary thing about it was the stark possibility of having to pursue a distant relationship if they come to an understanding to date and try to make it work. It was a tough choice and decision to make. Being in a relationship with someone across the Atlantic was no easy game. She had to let go of the bugging thought and freed her mind to just go ahead and enjoy the picnic and see what would become of it. And that was that.

Chapter Fourteen

ONE YEAR LATER

As usual with every year, soon after the New Year's celebration was over, springtime would come around while summer was knocking on the front door. Before you knew it, fall would be peeking from the back door. Soon it was November, and then they were going through the winter preps yet again.

Christmas then arrived as winter was steadily gaining steam. And luckily for that year, winter was quite kinder, and soon it had hastily passed on, giving way to the good weather just in time. Right at the edge of the spring, it was exactly one year since the dramatic anniversary of his fiancée's passing. He remembered the gigantic anaconda-sized snake and then the terrible nightmare that followed a day later. It was extraordinarily gut-wrenching. But that was in the past.

Fast forward, he imagined there wouldn't be a repeat of the previous year's crazy scenarios, but one never knew what was in the future. And because of that, he dressed up like a knight headed to battle. A week before that he had trained and sharpened his skills in all areas of his expertise. He did aerobics and jogged every morning, every day, as though he was preparing to fight something sinister and yet invisible. He fully knew that treading down the Valley of Death was sacred, ritualistic, and now scary as well.

Finally, the D-Day arrived. He collected all the items for the ceremony and whistled Gossiper to come: the candle, incense, and a matchbox, plus a little clay stand, saucer, and half glass of Locale drink, his late fiancée's favorite while she was alive.

They arrived fifteen minutes later. Archibald kept snapping his thumb and middle finger to indicate to Gossiper to stay alert and focused. He laid a white rug in the middle of the walk path and set the three candles and a tiny clay saucer in which he placed a piece of the incense and lit it with the burning stick of match beside the half glass of Locale drink. He observed his moment of silence that lasted for three minutes in deep meditation and dedication to his late friend's spirit.

Still in reverence, he opened his eyes just in time. He heard two people talking, and they seemed to be riding a motorbike at a slow speed. He looked back where he and Gossiper came from, looked up to the trees above, and then into the gaping mouth of the giant cave. The surprise—there wasn't anyone in sight!

"Hello there," he called out. The sound went dead, as if nothing happened. He scratched his head, thinking he was hallucinating. Well, maybe it never happened. He continued with his memorial service, spoke words to the spirit of his unseen wife-to-be, reciting the days and the good times that they had shared together, while Gossiper looked on.

With the candle burning, incense vaporizing a beautiful aroma within the under canopy of the jungle that covered the walk path overhead, an aura of access to a spiritual realm was established. Unbeknownst to Archibald, he was reaching out to another dimension that transcended the metaphysical world and existence. There was the tranquility and the reverence exuding from Archibald's inner self, which constituted a perfect environment for worship. Suffice it to say, an altar was in place. Archibald could feel the power of the captivating experience. It was surprising and nerving at the same time. The feeling scared him, and he was afraid of the control that seemed to overtake him.

He felt like he wasn't alone anymore. The feeling was far from the invisible motorbike that rode with two talking passengers across the roof of the forest above minutes ago. His hair stood erect on his skin. He wondered what the deal was because he was sure he no longer was alone, and yet whoever or whatever his companion was, he couldn't practically visualize! Gossiper started growling and exposing his canine teeth at the side of his mouth as though he'd seen an intruding cat. By that, Archibald confirmed his fears. Gossiper, too, saw and felt it, or whatever it was! They had company. An invisible company or intruder was within.

And then he heard something like footsteps coming from the cave, and then the next minute, there was a sound of wings flapping at the roof of the cave and flying toward the interior, away to the inner direction. Archibald kept turning around and scanning the environment around under the grass nearby, ready to fight back in self-defense.

"Hello there," Archibald broke the icy silence. "Come on out and show yourself," he bellowed again, using the sound of his voice as a weapon to sow fear and doubt in the approaching attacker, if any.

He turned back momentarily to look at his tiny altar; the candles had burned out, and to his utter disbelief, the glass of Locale, which was half full, was now empty! That was unbelievable! He was lost for words. Oh my gosh! And in a flash of Eureka, he realized what just happened. The correlation between his little altar, the burning candles with the incense, and the drink all constituted a bridge that connected the metaphysical world to the spiritual realm!

The big question was, whose spirit was it that descended there and drank the Locale? He vowed to find out. One way or the other. It wasn't going to be easy, but he'd have to try. The place quieted down to normalcy. and he could feel that too. He collected his ceremonial kits, and they trekked off out of the jungle.

Chapter Fifteen

A Day at the Anchorage

Like he did after surviving the deadly tornado, that night after the dramatic intercession with the spirits on behalf of his departed lady he did some long and hard thinking again. He wanted a complete and total evocation of the spirits that be, pull them out into the physical, material world of visibility, and take them on if necessary. That meant he needed a bunch of candles, incense, and everything he knew to make that plan effective.

The next morning he took a little trip down to the river. At Susitna River he did a quick, mission-driven fishing. Luck was on his side; he came out with five three-pound silver salmons, and those were enough to pay for the candles that he desperately needed. Next he headed to the hedge of the moorland overlooking Anchorage City that laid on the other side. Right at the fringes of the settlement he sold the salmons to a confidant whom he'd known over the years and replenished his supplies thereafter. Besides his much-needed ceremonial package, he was able to get some basic requirements as well. He headed back to the *Island of Tranquility*, the new name he'd coined for his abode. By the time he got to the cottage, the sun was already bidding farewell and soon the horizon would throw a curtain of darkness over the land on his side of the world.

He prepared his meal quickly, served Gossiper, and after having his fill, laid down to rest. He slept straight through the night—perhaps due to fatigue. After he woke up, he was greeted with familiar voices of chirping birds. He listened intently, as if trying to determine if it was his little guest, the robin, leading the chirpers that morning. *Nope, it must've been a bigger bird leading the choir of dawn,* he thought. He dropped the trivial thoughts and ran his mind over the plan he was about to execute later in the day.

After wrapping up breakfast consisting of hot potato and soup, he and Gossiper headed off to the Valley of Death. For some reason, he felt like it was his obligation to see "those things", whatever they were. He was ready to do that and expose their secrets to the world. But that required planning and strategizing, and he was up for the task.

Soon they were at it. They trekked on silently with occasional breaks when Archibald broke into a whistle of his favorite melody. He was a great whistler and he loved it because he thought it made him walk faster and forget any troubles that he might have.

Having reached the spot where he'd always performed his ceremonies, he passed it and headed straight to the mouth of the cave. He looked at Gossiper and assured him they were going in this time. He poked his head inside to do a little survey and made the first step. The iciness and the chilliness of the inside baffled him. It exposed the massive levels of glaciation and leaching that had taken place in this almost forbidden and fearsome arena. They advanced toward the interior where that winged, invisible creature had flown, flapping its gigantic imaginary wings that he could only hear the day before. He thought it sounded like one of those prehistoric reptiles that inhabited the earth alongside the dinosaurs several eons before the Neanderthals even trekked the earth. Squinting to acclimatize his eyes to the inside, he realized his effort wasn't working. The darkness heavily dominated the interior, and it was time to light his two flambeaux both of which he held in one hand.

The powerful light melted away the darkness from the cave

around him and Gossiper. They forged forward deeper and deeper into the bowels of the earth. Further and further he reached a point where stalactites had dripped down from the roof of the cave over the years, depositing sediments that formed tiny mountains of stalagmites rising from the floor of the cave, almost meeting with its source above. It was a spectacular pictorial. The air was dense and foggy, but there was no stopping now. They went on.

Almost a half a mile in or so, he found a flat surface over sheets of ice, planted the flambeaux at the side by pegging them down, and laid his bag's contents on the white snowy surface. He laid down the piece of rug, placed the candles on it, and twelve this time—no kidding! He went on to place half glass full of Localc drink and then the incense, which he lit up and started burning. The smoky characteristic smell of the incense billowed inside, and the aroma that exuded was more like a church altar prepping for a sacramental session. It was chilly, but thanks to the heat from the burning torches, he felt warmer and a little better; although it became even scarier down there. He occasionally warmed his hands over the burning torches and continued with his preps.

With all set, he calmed himself down and started his meditation and prayer. The atmosphere inside the cave became foggier with the trapped smoke from the flambeaux and the burning incense. He found himself uttering gibberish like a witch doctor doing an incantation to a god on behalf of a confessor. And then he sounded like he was talking to Matilda again. Soon the reality set in; the feeling of other invisible intruders around him filled the cave. He flashed thumbs up to Gossiper, as if to confirm and/or ask if he was aware of the new spiritual arrivals. He readied himself, unaware of how the encounter with the spirits would unfold. Friendly or belligerent, no one could tell. Then there was a deathly quietness in the arena. No sound, no wings flapping at the roof of the cave, and yet he knew they were not alone. He could feel it.

Luckily for Archibald, he was well prepared. The candles burned on, and he continued lighting one after the other to keep it going. He stayed in the spiritual realm long enough to confront and summon the spirits.

"Show yourself, come on out," he called out. "I want to see you. We can talk, you know."

Then the silence again. Not for long though. The same flapping of the wings like the other day came toward him from deeper in the cave, followed by a growl like from a lion, dragon, or a Godzilla of sorts! It lasted only for seconds, but it sounded angry and fierce. The sound grew closer and more threatening as sheets of broken stalactites were crumbling from the roof of the cave down on the sheet of the icy snow below. And there it was right in front of him, standing ten yards away from him, with an outline of smoke tracing its body size and shape, breathing monstrously. He drew his bow and arrow since he couldn't reach it with his newest superweapon, the close-combat sword.

Gossiper was growling the whole time by now. He aimed at what he perceived must have been its face as he could make from the smoky outline and released the weapon. Swoosh! Within seconds the arrow stopped motionless in midair right in front of the giant figure without any impact and fell to the ground! He drew another and released it yet again, surprisingly; he saw the real figure that stood before him! Approximately eight feet-tall, with powerful bat-like wings and red fiery eyes. It was like he showed himself only to demonstrate what was happening to his tiny arrows. He opened his right hand toward the arrow, and within a yard, it stopped midair. After seconds he waved it to the ground as though it was a harmless piece of stick.

And there was something else even more tantalizing, another giant. You probably guessed it—the giant anaconda snake that bit his neck in the nightmare a year ago! That was unbelievable. It was right there beside this massive, devilish figure, like a henchman of some sort to the heinous creature.

After the show of force, they both looked him straight in the eye as if to warn him, "Don't even try it," turned around, and as soon as it started flapping its wings, they both vanished off, turning into invisibility mode, and disappeared into the forbidden territory. What followed was a deathly silence in the cave.

Archibald was overwhelmed. He was defeated. Those creatures were unbeatable. Too powerful. Too gigantic and demonic. He collected his enchantment kits and waded off toward the exit. At least he saw it, or them. That was successful enough for him. He had wanted to see it or them for that matter, and he did. He tried to persuade himself to be happy and keep things positive, for at least from that point on, he knew what he was up against.

Chapter Sixteen

LIVING TO FIGHT ANOTHER DAY

"*He who fights and runs away may live to fight another day,*" Oliver Goldsmiths once said.

Archibald found himself boxed in a similar taunting situation from which he couldn't regress. And worse of all, it wasn't due to his own cowardice or fearfulness. From inside the cave he was ready for battle. In fact, he was already technically in battle, except that whatever weaponry he had were reduced to useless, obsolete toys by the monsters.

They had stood towering in front of him like a pair of Godzilla, totally unkillable. But for some reason, their sheer enormous sizes and statures didn't worry him, but the fact that his most formidable weaponry were all rendered ineffective gave him sleepless nights. He had to figure out a way to make another attempt to settle the score once and for all. "But how?" That was the question he asked himself minute after minute. He started simple by putting together a small metal workshop and began forging weapons of different types. He made three trips to the Anchorage area for supplies within three weeks—arrows, lassos, swords, machetes—and he also bought a rifle not only to remind himself of the fact he was a soldier once but most importantly because he needed firepower the next time he set foot inside that cave.

He customized his cartridges, bullets, swords, and all the weapons in his arsenal with a uniqueness akin only to them. All of them had a hallmark; one symbol in common etched on the tip meant to penetrate into the flesh of the enemy.

Next he went through the body protection strategies. With all options available, he forged customized armors for himself and for Gossiper too. After crafting the armors and refining them to a good fit, they did dress rehearsals and training—even more extensively than before. He was going to the battle of a lifetime. It wasn't just a carnal battle; it was a symbolic, spiritual battle with a physical dimension to it at the same time. If it meant being over prepared, so be it. He wasn't going to allow any tinge of complacency to influence him at all cost.

Finally, after several long, grueling days, the preps were over. He set a day off to rest and recuperate his spent energy. Prepared a sumptuous meal of peka with venison as the meat. He and Gossiper ate and, after having his fill, laid down to rest. The next day would be the ultimate confrontation with the devil himself. He had learned everything he could on strategies of fighting the kind of war he was faced with—a physical war with a spiritual dimension to it.

He woke up refreshed and energetic. The reality of his destiny stared at him in the face. That was the day he'd either live or die. If he died, at least he'd join Matilda in the afterlife. But if he attained victory by any stroke of luck and tact, it would be the pinnacle of his success, the culmination of his determination, hard work, training, and relentlessness coming in full circle in his defense of the territory that had become sacred to him. And Gossiper would be a towering figure in the story of that success. He was optimistic and nervous at the same time. At least it made him not to be complacent by any chance.

They loaded their stuff in the wheelbarrow and started off to the woods. As soon as they took the first steps, little fellow, the robin, was at it again at the same spot on the roof, starting his beautiful performance. It shot up straight into the air and descended back down on the roof. Archibald waved and bowed to him, and they hurried off toward the Valley of Death to go and kill or get killed by those monstrous creatures.

The good thing, though, was he could choose the time for the battle. And it was going to be at midday so that if there was going to be any dying, it'd be during the day, deep inside the cave. On reaching the walk path inside the forest domain, he knew they were at the contested arena already, and at that time, destiny would probably bring credibility to the name of the place, Valley of Death—a point of intersection between reality and conspiracy, so to speak.

They continued to the mouth of the giant, icy cave, at which point Archibald waved to Gossiper, and they were in. Ten yards in, and he lit the flambeaux again. They advanced deeper and deeper into the cave, moving as soundlessly as possible. On reaching the point where the monster made a mockery of his arrow a month ago, they headed on forward.

Archibald feasted his eyes again on the beauty of nature that graced this forbidden territory. The columns of calcium carbonate from the ceiling of the cave and its floor were still intact. But there was no time for admiration of art or nature now. He refocused on the battle ahead. The one thing he liked about that war was that he was the one to determine the time of attack whenever he was ready and in position. That gave him an edge in the battle.

For the fight to start, he had to evoke the spirits first; they never came uninvited unless it was in their specific interest. And so he set up the stage and put weapons in specific spots, planned everything that would be done during the fight. He positioned Gossiper at a ready spot and laid the enchantment kits all in place. Soon they were getting down to it. Candles lit and all set, he uttered words again, getting lost in the incantations and speaking to the spirits.

"Show yourselves, come on out, and face us!"

This time there were no wings flapping around like before, the reason being they'd set their altar pretty much in the middle of the party. He continued since he couldn't yet see anything to sling his modified weapons at. He was eager to see if he was right with his battle theories on evil from spiritual and physical perspectives.

The usual feeling that he was becoming accustomed to overshadowed them one more time, and he floated into the euphoria and the spiritual domain. Soon after that, it happened. It came in form of a deep growl and chest-thumping sounds. After that he heard a stampede-like sound arising from deeper in the cave, like a legion of army from the underworld, the army of the devil surging toward him and Gossiper. "This is it, Gossiper, this is it," he said out loud to his pal. He flipped down the cover of his helmet so he could only look through the thick glass. Minutes later they would be in a full-blown war.

Chapter Seventeen

Battle of the Titans

Archibald drew the first arrow, lit up the waxy tip, and released the weapon. His target—a six-foot-tall crucifix which he'd earlier planted in the far corner of the cave toward the interior. The waxed crucifix doused with gasoline caught fire instantaneously and illuminated the cave with a menacing spiritual symbolism of the spirit of good domineering over evil and darkness. The ripple effect was devastating to the army from hell. But that was just an opening shot and an onset of a fierce confrontation yet to come.

Within seconds Archibald had shot alight five crucifixes, and the inside of the cave was illuminated, more like a giant Cathedral set ablaze. The rebuttal came by way of a deafening, thunderous growl that shook the entire cave like a tremor of doom from the belly of the earth. Next was a simultaneous embodiment of all the spiritual forms into practical empirical forms in stark manifestations for Archibald to see. The two monsters led the band of wolf-like creatures.

That was the moment to try his shots on visible forms. There it was; ten yards away was the master of them all that he'd seen a month ago, the eight-feet-tall monster. Fast like lightening Archibald aimed his arrow, and swoosh! The arrow, laced with heavy dose of curare, was in the air, yards away from its target. Three, two, and quack! It didn't stop this time like the last, he hit the target! Right in the middle of its forehead, and he aimed another arrow, this time at the giant anaconda snake right beside the growling monster that was struggling to pluck off the arrow dangling on its forehead.

But he wasn't fast enough, just seconds after he had raised his arrow, the anaconda was no more in sight. It had instantly disembodied itself, vanishing into its invisible form. By descending into invisibility and nothingness, it attained a unique power of unpredictability of its position, and that was a major setback to Archibald.

Either way, he wasn't giving up or losing focus. He concentrated on the rest of the targets that he could still see. And there was one more thing he recognized; the powerful, winged giant monster was the titan among them, with absolute control over the rest. After a fierce struggle, the giant titan plucked off the arrow and vanished in seconds. He wished he'd planted another dose of the nerve-poisoning curare with a second arrow instead of aiming at the anaconda, but that was a lost chance now. It turned out the monster had lost its power of disembodiment momentarily because of the sticking arrow on its head.

The fight was gaining steam again. There was another growl blowing strong air currents on each of the five burning crucifixes and dimming off the flames with darkness, imminently threatening to blanket the inside of the dark cave. Archibald saw that, and he wasn't letting it happen. Fast as he could, he plucked two arrows, lit them up with the candle lights that were still burning, and released the shots one after the other, relighting the giant crucifix and another around the middle section of the cave. The lights came on just in time for Archibald to see Gossiper swept off his feet by the invisible monster in midair, which was the master titan in action. He could trace the outline of its body by the movement of Gossiper in midair. He determined the possible exact position of its head. This time he was tipping the arrow with fire and gasoline. *Whoosh!* It hit its target, and the giant creature reappeared; and at the same time, the rest of the fighting legions wallowed in pain for their master as if they, too, could feel his pain at the same time.

Another arrow, again with fire on it, shot through its heart. Finally, he gave up on Gossiper and let him off its powerful grip. Gossiper fell off from several yards off the ground onto the sheet of ice below, his body armor clanking as he thudded to rest. Luckily, only his left forelimb was sprained from the devil's tight grip. The monster was losing control now; it tottered like a drunken giant, walking with swollen, fractured legs, totally uncoordinated.

Archibald fired two shots from his gun at its head just to crush the skull and inflict more damage. The rest of the gang started retreating deeper and deeper into the cave, but the giant anaconda remained a few yards away, wriggling as if in pain. That was Archibald's next target. He was so outraged by it and wanted to settle their differences in battle immediately.

But for a start, he had to finish the leader first. In a Japanese Kenjutsu swordsmanship fighting style for close combat, Archibald drew his long sword, surged forward, swung the sword frantically, and chopped off the monster's left wing just to make sure he would not fly away this time. The monster growled with his red fiery eyes glued on Archibald. It was not its fiery gaze that would stop Archibald from surging forward and fighting, but something else did—his name!

"Archie, help me!"

He was transfixed! He darted off from the wallowing monster so he wouldn't give himself away due to the distraction from the unknown caller. Once at a safe distance, he looked around to investigate and see who in that hell of a cave of demons knew his name. Thinking perhaps he was hallucinating, he stopped and spun round to look at Gossiper if he'd for some reason become a *talking dog* in that demonic territory and called him by name. Nope! It wasn't Gossiper. Then he looked at the fallen titan, still wallowing on the sheet of ice, puking a greenish, yellow fluid that tainted the white snow, as if green slimy algae were poured on it.

He saw something else; the giant anaconda snake was looking different now, like some kind of a mermaid fish with a humanlike face. To his utter astonishment, that was what had called his name! Something else he realized was, the weaker the dying titan got, the clearer and more revealing the face of the mermaid became. Whenever the titan lifted its head, as if it was getting revived, the mermaid's head turned back into the perfect head of a snake. At that point, Archibald knew what he had to do to test his hypothesis. He drew his sword again, chopped the legs off, then the right wing, and rendered it wingless. The arms came next, and finally he exposed its trunk. Then the neck required his powerful machete.

Immediately the mermaid called him again, "Archie, it's me, M-m-matilda!"

Chapter Eighteen

Reincarnation

As the greenish bloodlike fluid gushed out of its huge veins, life and power drained out from the giant creature minute after minute. Archibald looked on, and what he saw was clarity displayed before him.

The identity of what he had known as his enemy number two, the anaconda snake, *"Matilda,"* finally became unmistakably clear.

"It's me, Archie, it's me!" she called out again.

No one else called him that way that he could remember except his mom when he was still a little boy.

Still bamboozled and skeptical, thinking he was being fooled, he looked quizzically at the snake-turned-human, and there it was, another proof of her identity. As the giant monster died slowly and surely, Matilda stood up now, exactly like her real self, unmistakable and with her absolute beauty as the true Matilda that he had once known and befriended. She was his wife-to-be, reborn!

By then, the burning crucifixes were dimming off, and Archibald lit up the last two of the flambeaux so he could behold the strange figure that stood before him—Matilda from another world. Could that be a doppelganger of the true Matilda he knew, or was she the one and only authentic Matilda? All he could do was just wonder and look at the incredible unfolding in front of him. She was coming back to life, getting reincarnated before his very eyes…it was unbelievable.

Scared, confused, and ecstatic at the same time, Archibald stood speechless, out of moves. His next move was to destroy the snake that now stood before him as his ex-girlfriend and fiancée, the snake that bit his neck in a dream, scaring the heck out of him a year ago was his life partner.

"What the heck happened?" He shook his head to regain his focus as the words spewed out of his mouth.

"It's a long story, darling, but first, let's make sure it never happens again," Matilda responded. "Come with me," she called Archibald and Gossiper.

"By the way, meet my dog, the only friend I had since you left, Gossiper!"

"Aww, that's nice."

"Gossiper, here's Matilda."

They followed her lead deeper inside the cave.

"Come before he wakes up," she cautioned. "He's not dead yet. I'll show you. We've got to finish the job."

Deeper and deeper they advanced into a far corner of the cave, heading to what she called the main nest where the life source was protected. They left the giant creature fighting for its life and wriggling on the floor of the cave where the battle had raged moments ago. It was rolling blindly like a bull whose head was severed and left to kick its life away as it rolled over into the next world.

Like two hundred yards inside, they entered into a corner with compartments that looked like some kind of a shrine. She led them to pots that contained some embryonic life-forms that stood in rows of three, a total of nine.

"This is it! The life source of that giant creature. Give it four to five hours. It would reassemble all its body parts together, walk back here, and swallow one of these"—she motioned her hand over the pots—"and it'd be totally renewed! Stronger and more energized as if nothing you did out there ever happened to it!"

She took Archibald's machete, broke one pot after another, and each time she did that, there was a tremor and a growl from the creature in the far end of the cave toward the exit where it was left to finally die. Archibald joined in and broke the last two pots, and with all the embryos out, they split them all up to make sure they were kaput, 100 percent. Finally, they doused the inside of the nest with the last bit of gasoline Archibald had left and lit up the final flame in there to wrap up a mission that was almost destined to be impossible and left hurriedly.

They jogged back toward the exit, found the creature totally shriveled by now like a rotten piece of skin on the ice.

"See." Matilda pointed to it. "It's finally over!"

They collected the last of their weapons and headed out of the dungeon as quickly as they could.

Archibald couldn't still believe what happened. It was beyond his wildest dreams. He got more than he ever hoped for, more than he bargained for.

"No way! This is crazy, you know?" he said to her.

"I know, right? And I tried everything I could to signal to you who I was with the little power he'd left me with. I so badly wanted you to know what I was, but it wasn't easy. But I am so glad you felt connected to me in some unexplainable, mysterious ways even though it almost seemed impossible given the circumstances! Now I am so happy you came back for me. I would have been forever lost if it wasn't for you, Archibald. That, I am sure of. You are so brave and unrelenting. I think that's why I befriended you."

"Just so we're clear, can I see under your left breast," Archibald asked.

There it was. She lifted her left breast to expose a tiny half-inch tattoo of a cross, which she'd gotten on her eighteenth birthday to conceal an ugly-shaped birthmark which she didn't like. That was the final irrefutable proof Archibald needed to believe it was her.

"Do you believe now?" She asked him as they walked back to the cottage.

"One hundred percent," he replied.

Chapter Nineteen

SO WHAT HAPPENED?

The whole story revolved around the greenery, the flowers, and the dunes at the riverside—all too beautiful and attractive to stay away from.

"I always created reasons to justify my presence at the river so I could walk on the sand and feel the breeze over my skin," Matilda explained. "You loved to hunt, and I couldn't stop or blame you for your passion or deny you the opportunity to enjoy what you loved. I had to let you do it, but at the same time, I had to find something meaningful while you were always gone to pass time, you know. Do you remember the day I told you I was going to collect firewood down the river? You were on your way down to check the bird traps. I still remember it because that was when everything about this whole saga started." She paused momentarily and went on with her narrative.

"Well, after you left to go, I dressed up in my tiny little red velvety top and moseyed down to the valley into the river with hype and gusto, like an athlete training for the world title in her passionate sport. While there, I was consumed in the activities and was without any care in the world. Later I collected firewood, and when I was ready to go, I met a man who greeted me and asked me to help him lift a piece of log, which he said he wanted to use. When I told him I was in a hurry and wanted to get home as quickly as I could, he insisted and told me there was something else he wanted to ask of me again, and he said he wanted me as a close friend. I told him I was betrothed and soon to be married and that friendship with him wasn't going to be possible. He firmly told me he meant whatever he said and that he was giving me three days to respond positively. He was harassing me literally, and that's what I told him." Archibald listened intently with a grin on his face.

"But I assured him there wasn't going to be any need for the three days because I was never going to meet him again. After all, I didn't know him, and he didn't know me. He said I might not know him, but it was inaccurate to assume that he didn't know me, 'the only woman living in the riverside whom he saw anytime he wanted.' And so, he said, 'See you in three days, Matilda!' and left.

"I was stunned, especially when he mentioned my name. It was so brazen of him, but I brushed it off, thinking he could've heard my name any one of those crazy days that we called each other while playing at the river."

"For two days I treated the issue like a joke from a rude and crazy man. That was why I didn't tell you about the incident. But I did promise myself to tell you if I saw him again or if he dared set foot on our compound at the cottage. For the two days that followed, I never made it easy for him even though I wasn't sure he would even dare. I stayed at the cottage the whole time, never getting anywhere near the river or down to the valley. And then on the fateful day, I was inside, serving dinner, when you stepped outside to take a quick bath. At that moment, I saw someone enter in through the door and thought it was you returning from your bath. In shock, only to realize it was him!"

"Instinctively, I yelled, of course, to the top of my lungs, but he put his index finger on his lips and shooed me off, but I continued to yell anyways. Unbelievably, his index finger on his own lips muffled off my voice, and no matter how hard I tried or what I did, I couldn't get a single word out to you."

"Immediately he grabbed my hands, and within seconds I

realized he wasn't human! The scales on the palm of his hands felt like the bark of a tree on my wrists. Instantly out of my control, my eyes closed, and the next time they opened, we were at the Valley of Death, alone! Thoughts ran through my mind, and I regretted why I never told you about it, but it was too late. And then he told me he could read my thoughts and knew about my resistance directed at him, and for that, he had no choice but to kill me."

"But then he said it would be unfair not to give me an offer if I wanted to live by any chance."

"Do you want to live or die?" He asked me.

"At that point, my voice came back, and guess what my first utterance was… 'Archie, help me!' Unfortunately, I couldn't even say the first complete word audibly before he muffled my vocal cords off, forever!"

"And then he said, 'I see you haven't appreciated getting your voice back. From now on, your voice is off as long as I live, and you'll soon learn that's pretty much forever! Time for using gestures and signs then,' he directed.

"And so I started to use signs and nodded or shook my head to communicate my intentions.

He told me he could only keep me alive in any one of two forms—as a dragon or as a giant anaconda. Immediately to illustrate his point, he snapped his thumb and middle finger, and instantly I shifted form into an ugly dragon with red fiery eyes. The next minute, before I could recover from the astonishment, he snapped again, and I turned into the giant anaconda that you've seen many times. The third snap put me back into my real self for the last time before I decided which direction I wanted to go morphologically. He then asked me to decide immediately lest I'd be dead in sixty seconds. That was the lowest moment of my entire life, I guess. It was like being asked which of your two parents you would kill or get killed yourself. Something almost impossible to do or imagine. Well, I did it anyway, and I was a snake."

"And then he said had I chosen to be a dragon, I would have automatically become his wife, but since I became a snake, he'd respect my choice and only make me his righthand 'person', or should I say creature, to do his bidding. From that time on, I did everything as a snake, but I still had my conscience and personhood invisibly buried within me. I also had other powers that I could use to do things for him. For instance, I could send dreams to people, send signals through animals, birds, but the most painful thing was I couldn't speak."

"So over the years I designed a plan to provoke you into action and coerce you by carefully goading you to fight the battle that you fought because I saw that as the only slim possibility of my survival and possible reincarnation. Thank heavens it worked! The first design of my master plan was that confrontation, and so I had to shed my giant snakeskin right in the place where you always performed your ceremony to attract your attention and then intentionally crawl into the cave to entice you inside."

"I realized you had never considered going in there, and so I had to lead you to it. The nightmare was to challenge you to do more because I knew what you were up against."

"Wow!" Archibald finally found his voice to speak. "You were more like a goddess torching the way for me and Gossiper, weren't you?"

"Sort of. But remember I was the one in need of help, and that didn't make me the most powerful goddess, did it?" she responded. "You were the one looming so large in the whole battle triangle generally. A force to reckon with, so to speak. Even though I knew the monster was powerful, I believed in you more and knew you would be able to conquer it with time. It was worth a try, and so I took the chance."

That evening they spoke about the old times, the memories, and the time they lost as fiancé and fiancée who were headed for a happy married life. For dinner, it was a special meal. Like you already guessed, it was peka with pheasants to welcome the new arrival. It was like she was back from hell to life. Archibald was trying hard to get used to the reality and the fact of his newly revitalized life, a twist like no one could've expected in a millennium. He couldn't have been luckier with Matilda right beside him and Gossiper, too, at the cottage.

The next morning, while eating breakfast, Matilda asked Archibald how he came to learn about the cross-symbol tricks and all the craziness about the crucifixes. She laughed at how desperation to win the battle had made him so capricious and unpredictable and was surprised he pulled it off without much help from her.

In her mind she had thought she was going to defect during the battle and, with the powers she'd harnessed from the beast, join forces with Archibald and together slay the monster. She didn't have to do that with Archibald's war plan so successful in the end.

Chapter Twenty

THE FLAMING COTTAGE

One afternoon an Alaskan airline pilot flying the old Douglas DC-6 spotted something peculiar in the Alaskan countryside at the foot of the mountains down below as they approached Anchorage City a few miles away: a tiny ball of flame that looked like a ripe bright-orange coconut fruit patched on the vast greenery below.

Down on the ground, Archie and Matilda had made a decision. Time had come for them to backtrack from the most adventurous life they'd ever embarked on as a couple. They had abandoned everything normal and regular and gone on an extraordinary expedition in the jungle and in the process discovered incredible creativity, resilience, and talents they had no idea were in the imprint of their DNA blueprint. Archibald never knew he could shoot through an orange thrown in midair twice with arrows before it landed on the ground.

For Matilda, even though she'd gone to school for catering, she had no idea she was such a talented kitchen gardener and a fine fisherwoman too. She managed her vegetables and maintained a steady supply for their little family all year round.

However, with those exciting highlights also came other dangerous twists and experiences, which threatened their very existence. They were lucky to have survived the island, but it was a thriller and a killer all at the same time, and so, no regrets.

But with all said and done, they wanted to move on back to civilization, back to where they truly belonged, among the people and with the people. When they reached that decision, they realized they had a huge problem with it: procrastination. They just continued staying there, one day after another. Each day they'd say, "We'll leave tomorrow." And then they'd do the same the next day. The whole thing was like a continuous tale of tomorrow tied to the next tomorrow, forever. It was one month after agreeing to let go of the jungle that they started making a real move. Archibald dug a trench around the cottage, heaping the dirt to form a mound around it as though he was creating an animal barricade.

The next day that followed he collected water from the river, each time pouring in the trench around the house. And then on day three, with all their portable belongings packed in one lift off bag, they painfully torched the only cottage in the mountain foot.

"It's like a tiny ball of fire down there," a pilot had said. "I wonder how the fire is keeping itself in check exactly like a disciplined wolf among lambs in the middle of the jungle and not spreading around elsewhere," he'd observed to his copilot.

Down below Archibald knew why. He'd to make sure the fire did only what it was meant to do, and so he had to customize, design, and monitor it every step of the way. Once the cottage had completely burned down, they had no choice but to leave their home of almost eight years. Archibald made sure the embers had completely died off by sprinkling water over what was left, and with no any fizzling, he was satisfied the fire was gone.

Before they left, they cleaned up and groomed themselves as best they could before rejoining society again. Finally, they left on their bikes, Matilda riding for the first time in years. It was going to be a journey of three hours to the Anchorage area, where they'd lived in a rented apartment years ago. When they arrived, Archibald knocked on the door of his long-term pal and confidant.

Larry Doolittle opened the door, and he couldn't believe his eyes!

"Guys! Are you from the moon, or am I dreaming? Come on, you." He grabbed Archibald and hugged him and then Matilda, whom he'd briefly met before they went to their ill-fated picnic years ago. "Come in and make yourselves comfortable."

Doolittle offered them a place to stay until they got back on their feet again.

Matilda couldn't take her eyes off from Doolittle's beautiful, artistic wall. There were four crucifixes of different sizes lined up with approximately equidistant between each pair. There were other spectacular artworks too. There was a landscape painting of a mountainous scenery, probably of Alaska, she thought. And then there was the masterpiece in the center of the wall: the basilica of ancient Rome. It was an excellent feast for the eyes. And she helped herself to it. She was quietly carried away in the imaginary world while engrossed in art appreciation.

Once she got a chance, she pointed to the crucifixes and smiled at Archibald, as if to remind him to explain the coincidence with what happened in the cave on the day of the battle.

He nodded his head and said, "Yeah, it was him. I came here for advice while preparing for the assault, you know. He is deep in those spiritual ideologies and suggested if my fight was more than carnal, which it was, then I would do better to use spiritual symbols in combat. He also advised on the use of the nerve agent, curare, that I had personally not considered. And so he was part of my war planning crew and a combat partner in proxy," Archie concluded.

Just as he did so, Mr. Doolittle entered the living room with two bottles of Kella rose, red mountain wine, in his hand to celebrate the reunion. They drank to good health and friendship and talked about a wide range of issues. At one point, Archibald teased his host whether he was a sworn celibate for life.

"Ha ha ha, you never give up, do you? Well, someday, maybe when things settle down here. Maybe the next time you guys return from one of those crazy voyages of yours, I should be a complete man. Did you say you were planning another gig to where was it again?" he asked, waving to Archibald.

"Galapagos Island," Archie replied. "I hear that's a natural paradise for living organisms. Charles Darwin should tell you more about that sometime if you read his theories of evolution," he concluded.

Chapter Twenty-One

THE UNBROKEN POT

For the first time in years Matilda looked at herself in the mirror after a complete and normal shower in a tub, and she couldn't believe what she went through. It was unfathomable that she was alive and out of a dire situation from which she'd felt completely irredeemable for years until just a few days ago. She tried to wrap her head around the ordeal with the monster, its systems in the cave, the battle, and then she remembered something, the special pot of the life-saving embryos. There was the one pot with double layer in the far corner that required to be broken twice to smash out the embryo. Then she recalled that it was Archie who finished that one in the corner.

By only breaking the outer layer, it meant it was actually unbroken in the real sense, and that meant they probably had a real problem in their hands.

She hated to think of it, but now she realized there was 1 percent possibility that the monster could actually get revived. Just 1 percent—not much, but something. The problem was she wasn't sure and not ready to go back there anywhere within a mile's radius from the cave, within which in the event that the monster was alive, by a slim chance, then its powers could reach her and likely turn her back into the anaconda form. She needed to check that by any means possible in order to free herself from that worry.

Looking at her skin that was already regaining its original, youthful glow made her cringe at the possibility that the monster could still be alive. The thought that its death was now not 100 percent guaranteed poked a deep hole in her sense of happiness.

Once she was out of the bathroom, she asked Archibald if he recalled how the last pot in the corner was crushed. His response was even more disturbing. He recalled that the pot simply peeled off to expose a second layer, and he thought that was it. And by the time he saw that, they had already doused the place in gasoline and lit the flame to burn down the nest area.

"I thought the flame would finish the job, so I just ran outside with you. Is that something I should worry about?" he had enquired.

"I think so," she replied. "I think we just lost the one hundred percent level of certainty that the monster was totally eliminated, that's all. We now stand at ninety-nine percent, which is pretty good. The one percent is a sheer probability, so I guess we should relax and enjoy the life now," she concluded and tried to brush off the worry.

*　*　*

It was 5:45 p.m. when Matilda returned from the floral shop where she worked. She always arrived five minutes plus or minus 5:30 p.m. After her arrival, she routinely dropped her purse on the lone loveseat in the middle of their tiny studio apartment and walked straight into the bathroom for a shower, which lasted seven minutes.

Stuck to her routine as always, she walked out of the shower after seven minutes and thirty seconds.

As she stepped out, "Surprise!"

Archibald was right there in front, right knee on the floor with a tiny maroon ring box in his left hand, with the right hand popping the box half-opened to expose a glittering diamond engagement ring. Surprised and dumbfounded, she screamed and gaped with eyes alight with excitement.

"Oh my gosh!" she exclaimed.

Archibald was just smiling, and then he spoke, "Seven years ago I asked you, and you said, 'Yes, but not now.' Today, after all the dramatic life that we've all gone through, the survival and all, what will your answer be, my dear Matilda Juergen? Will you do me the honors?"

She extended her left hand so Archie could plant the ring where it belonged. As he did so, tears welled in her eyes as she choked with emotion emblematic of happiness.

"Yes!" She finally let out an ecstatic answer that Archibald had longed to hear for a long time.

That night they had dinner in a fancy restaurant to celebrate their engagement. By the time they returned home, they had set a wedding date, which was just weeks away. Their dating period was long gone with the years, and they had waited long enough.

* * *

She wore a draping, silky, light creamy dress designed like the popular maxis of the 1950s falling over her feet. Her gold laced leather shoes with slightly raised heel completed the final touch to a stylistically attired lady of class ready to walk down the aisle. The irony, though, was that the aisle in their case was to be the grass at the banks of Susitna River in Matanuska. The background was the sparkling water of the river and all that came along with nature.

You probably guessed right; they chose to wed at the riverbanks where they had spent the earlier days of their then budding love life seven years ago. Archibald wore a steely gray tuxedo with a peacock tail that extended down to the ankle like for a hospital clown. The wedding ceremony took exactly twenty minutes, with only six guests in attendance. As they stood for their picture, they chose the oceanic background to make a statement about their romantic taste.

Behind them was a simply constructed arch carved out of fresh wooden poles with twining flowers coiling through the entire length of the semicircle, which was all Mr. Doolittle's idea. As if to grace the scene from above, a couple of albatrosses flew leisurely overhead as if to predict great success in their married life. About ten yards away to the side stood a brown horse with a simple wagon, ready to wheel off the newlyweds to their honeymoon spot soon after the ceremony was completed. Their destination, yes, like you might have predicted, was in Anchorage Hotel, room 24, the very spot representing the genesis of their enduring love. They were booked for three nights, and as a courtesy, the hotel had extended it to free seven-day package of VIP treatment to the lovebirds.

Chapter Twenty-Two

WAITING IN DESPAIR

Like she was trained by her mother from childhood, Matilda stuck to the rules of effective family communication in her early years with her parents whenever she was away from home. Her mother steadfastly required her to call them at home at least once within two days whenever she was away from home. She recalled long ago—a decade perhaps—while in Frankfurt, visiting her paternal uncles and cousins after her parents left a week earlier, returning to Zagreb so she could remain and attend a concert in which two of her cousins were participants, she called them every other day to keep in touch. That was her mom's golden rule, which, according to her, kept everyone in the family at ease, knowing they were all safe. Her father did the same, and so did she.

And when she kissed her goodbye at Frankfurt Airport a week before she boarded the plane to Alaska, her mom leaned close and whispered a line in her ears that went like, "remember the golden rule, sweetheart. It keeps everyone at ease." She smiled and released her to go into the world. Matilda had made it a pledge to do that, and it was second nature. For that she always kept in touch, knowing should it happen for her not to call in three days, her mother would be shouting, "mayday, mayday," on the mountaintop. With that in mind, the moment she arrived at Anchorage Hotel, she did perfectly well by calling her people almost daily.

On the day of her planned picnic with her new friend, she called her mother before they left the hotel and hoped to call immediately on returning after three days. She specifically told her mom the picnic would last three days minimum. That same day she also placed another call to the airlines, letting them know she was having an extended vacation and would want her return date postponed until after two weeks. For the change, she was required to pay additional fee to seal the deal.

After her booking at the hotel expired, cash ran down, and she and Archibald took their relationship to another level; meanwhile the airlines told her in order to reschedule the return flight, she needed to pay almost half the total flight cost, which she didn't have on hand, and her return date was already gone. Archibald promised her he'd help and look around for a return ticket to Zagreb after things settled. She was told after one week it would have to be full booking fee for the return ticket. Time wasn't on her side. With countless people arriving in the United States and sometimes overstaying their visas, when it clocked six months after Matilda's visa was officially over, her status still indicated she was in the country. The immigration office made checks and inquiries to establish her whereabouts, but her traces disappeared with no additional reports from the hotel. The only person of interest was Archibald, who was assumed to be her boyfriend; but since he, too, was missing, there was nothing to be done about the case, and the file was marked "unresolved" and pushed to the back.

* * *

Matilda's parents knew something wasn't right when she ceased calling altogether. She was well trained and knew the rules even though she was already twenty-one and an adult. She was still a part of their family and a part of their life, forever, and there was no reason in the world she was going to abandon the communication habit with them that was well established as their family tradition from her childhood. On their part, they called the immigration office and Customs on a weekly basis for six months, and each time they were told the same thing: the case was being looked into. There were no leads so far. After six months, they expected the worst news, but no news came. No new information. Just stone dead silence. They grew angry and devastated.

For some time, whenever anyone walked into their family house, they'd see nothing but gloom written on their faces. They were barely getting by. It was like their world had come to a standstill. The grief was unbearable, and they knew they might never hear from or see her again. It was unbelievable how a wonderful gift of love turned out to be the genesis of the worst tragedy their family would ever know. By the time it was about to clock one year since her disappearance, they had to do what they were required to do. They could no longer ignore it. Facing the truth was inevitable. They went together to the post office where they would make their final definitive phone call to the American authorities and make a final judgment for the sake of their daughter. They had to accept it; she was gone, and they had to summon whatever little courage they had left to face that truth, honor her legacy, and pay their respects to her at least with a decent funeral. It was an unspeakable, heartbreaking horror, but it had to be done.

As expected of the phone call, the case was still unresolved like before, and there were no leads. According to the Customs officials, at the one-year anniversary, if nothing turned up, they were going to reclassify it as a "cold case" and archive the file.

During that last call, they made a final request to the Customs officials if they wouldn't mind calling and alerting them if anything turned up by the one-year mark, which was eight days away, so they would delay her planned memorial service in case of any prospects that she could still be alive.

In case they didn't call, they would automatically assume there was nothing to wait for and go ahead and hold the symbolic memorial prayer that they were preparing.

Two days after the one-year mark, there was a somber scene at Mirogoj Cemetery, located to the north side from the center of Zagreb City. Beautiful with spectacular scenery, the magnificent memorial park held many secrets of pain, extraordinary legacies, and love of countless individuals who now rested underneath the earth in the vast estate of the late Ljudevit Gaj, a departed leader of the Croatian people of former Yugoslavia. In the background stood the towering mountains of Medvednica whose shadows devotedly covered the graveyard in the evenings on a daily basis like a promise that would always be kept forever.

Matilda's was one intriguingly unique case that left her parents and relatives grappling with hypotheticals and reality that were clearly unresolvable in the short term. She was an individual whose life would be memorialized on the grounds of Mirogoj by her loved ones while her body laid elsewhere, transatlantic, a land unknown to her people. Her casket would be devoid of her remains but full of her beautiful memories and the spectacular life that she had lived. That was her fate, a thing you would want to change but simply couldn't. Tears rolled, and faces were wiped. Sobs and anguish and mourning went on at the graveyard.

Twenty mourners conferred in the multidenominational burial grounds to undertake a memorial interment of a young, beloved daughter of the community and a friend whose memory and legacy they cherished world without end. On Matilda's symbolic epitaph, there were these inscriptions:

> *You left us without a word, but we know and feel you now lay in the ground somewhere in this earth unknown to us.*
>
> *We want you to know we had a special place for you here. Should we ever locate your remains, we will bring you home where you belong.*

We will never stop looking for you nor shall we ever forget the love we shared while you were here in our midst.

With eternal love from the city of Zagreb, your home.

Inside the symbolic casket were her favorite childhood dolls and a few clothes. For the first time in six months, after assuming she'd died and would never return, Matilda's parents ate a proper meal, spent the evening normally in their living room with a few close relatives and friends, and shared her memories in photos and letters with a sigh of relief of letting go of the overwhelming burden that had weighed heavily on them.

Going through the funeral ceremony might have been heavily depressing on them, but it was also relieving in the end as they came to discover. They experienced the turnaround and began to see a purpose for their life again as a couple. That all came at a price—accepting the truth of the loss. It was like the biblical story of King David who fasted for days, wore sackcloth, and covered himself in ashes and dust, pleading for the life of his son, Daniel, who was critically ill. When Daniel died, David ended his fast and cleaned himself. The servants wondered why. His answer was, there was no need to punish himself anymore because his son was gone. He accepted the truth, and that gave him the relief and the opportunity to hit the reset button and move on. Matilda's parents reluctantly but surely punched on their reset button and started afresh.

The following day they decided to travel to Frankfurt so they could spend some time with the relatives of Matilda's father for a while. They thought changing the environment could help with their recovery from the depressing moments they had gone through and endured.

Chapter Twenty-Three

TEARS OF A MOTHER

In the thick and thin, everything came down to the powers beyond her means and control. The years had flown by fast in almost-lightning speed, and she'd lost control over her humanity while trapped in the mysteriously animated, magical world of the monsters that she'd for years become a part of against her willpower. Matilda realized that the path she was forced to walk had eroded her good spirit and sense of judgment gradually, and it was only until after she miraculously came back to life—thanks to Archibald's courage, fight, and resilience—that she'd given much thought about her true family, the suffering they must've gone through, and what she could do to make amends, if it was even possible. It was a fight that she was willing to take on again, a fight to gain back what she used to have and be—her real, authentic self.

Looking into her soul, she realized it was not only her stubbornness that prompted her hesitation to jump on the next flight to Zagreb after her rescue so she could show herself to her mother and family, but it was more complex than that. From the beginning of her friendship at the hotel, her failure to call her mother for three full weeks during the extraordinary picnic with Archibald had already created an initial angst within herself out of an unintended consequence of making a rushed commitment in a relationship, which oftentimes befell the youngsters whenever they stumbled in love for the first time. It was sheer negligence that only a teenager and/or a young adult understood and yearned for their elders to perceive, but in vain, a supposedly frustrating generational disconnect that no one could clearly explain.

It was therefore clear and understandable where her frustration and hesitation to confront her parents originated from. Even during their grand preparations to go to Galapagos, she ostensibly chose to live behind the canopy of truth and reality denying the responsibility that fell squarely on her laps and no one else's. No one was going to face her parents for her except her. That was just the plain truth. To bury her head in the sand like a dumb ostrich wasn't going to cut it any longer.

Once it was one month left to the planned trip into the unknown Galapagos Island, that truth hit home. She couldn't live in lies anymore. She was her mother's daughter and her father's lifeline, daughter, and friend. She had to ask for their forgiveness above all else. Like the biblical prodigal son reached his breaking point, she, too, had to face her own demons and flaws and confront them head-on.

"I will rise and go to my father and mother and kneel before them and tell them, 'I have wronged you beyond imagination and…'" She couldn't believe the emotions behind that confessional thinking, and tears rolled down her cheeks as though it was a real confession to her parents. She was stunned but relieved now that she was ready and decided to wind back the clock and return to the beginning. She wiped off the tears from her face down to her cheeks, and before she could sober herself to normalcy, Archibald entered the room and caught her crying.

"What's going on, sweetie?" he asked, taking her hand in his and raising her cheek so he could look into her eyes.

She sobbed uncontrollably before she could bring herself to explain the nagging issue. Archibald agreed and promised to help her resolve the issue.

* * *

Two weeks later Maria Juergen, Matilda's mother, was doing her normal chores in their Sesvete home, moving up and down, in and out of the house, cleaning the living room. She walked out with a tray on which she had placed two glasses half-filled with pale-yellow orange juice that she was taking to the side shade where they always took breaks and relaxed during sunny days. Her husband was just coming out of the bathroom, still wrapped in a white towel. As she stepped out, she suddenly stopped, transfixed like she'd stepped on a thick wood glue barefoot and trapped to the ground. The tray fell from her hands, as though she had gotten paralyzed in an instant from the shoulders down to the fingertips of both hands. The juice spilled over, and the glasses disintegrated into fragments and splinters on the tiled pavement in seconds.

Her head swirled in slow motion as she dropped on her knees, being careful to evade the shattered glass splinters at the side, tears rolled down her face, speechless. The tears of a compassionate mother flowed profusely down on the tiles. She was in shock and disillusionment, unable to utter a single word. Only her tears could communicate her feelings, which were a mixture of unexplainable emotions. Right in front of her stood Matilda Juergen, her supposedly dead daughter. Matilda herself couldn't talk, at least for a while. She finally found her words.

"I am so sorry, Mom. I am so sorry. I don't deserve your forgiveness and love, neither do I deserve your care because I have disobeyed you and all the good training that you have taught me…" She confessed with tears rolling down her face. Emotions were running high.

Her mother placed her left hand over her heart and raised her right hand toward her daughter, as if to reach out to her. Matilda came forth, knelt beside her mother, embracing, and both women cried in each other's arms. Her father rushed out to check what was going on, towel flying off from his waist—revealing a pair of green shorts—and he barely noticed that the towel was gone. He joined the two ladies in a kneeling embrace and harmonized with the crying party as well. For minutes they spoke no words, just cried. It was like the fact of her being alive was more important than any reason whatsoever. She was alive, after all, and that was the only thing that mattered to them in the wide world.

When the drama was finally over, her parents promptly told her, "we forgive you no matter what happened. The stories of your adventures will not influence our decision to forgive you. We love you unconditionally and are forever grateful for a second chance to love you again while you are alive and physically with us."

"My stories are unbelievable, but hopefully, I'd be able to share them sometime," she responded. "I love you guys so much."

They hugged again and walked to the living room, holding each other's hands. As they settled, her mom brought a jar of orange-juice leftover and poured each one a glass.

They raised the glasses and toasted, "To reincarnation and reunion."

Cheers. Cheers. Cheers. They talked and caught up on how the relatives were doing, and then the friends.

"Mia, by the way, is married and with two kids already!" her mother told her.

"Wow! Now that makes me realize I have been away for a darn long time!" Matilda replied. "Is she anywhere here in Zagreb?" she inquired.

"Yes, she is. A few minutes from the city, on the south side," her mom answered. "I know what you're thinking, but just relax. You'll see everybody."

* * *

Matilda called Archibald on the phone and let him know all was fine, confirming at least they were able to pull off the trip, and all her parents were settled now. She and Archibald had to do a lot of explaining to the Customs authorities, and even though they listened, they didn't seem to have believed all they had to say. But at least they received payment of fine for overstaying her visa. After purchasing a return ticket, she decided that calling anyone and giving notification that she was alive wouldn't be a good idea, considering what her parents' reaction would be, and so she also requested the Customs officials to let her go and do the notification during the reunion herself. After that, she just boarded the plane and went on with the journey, which ended at her parents' doorstep.

The two weeks that followed Matilda had to go through lengthy processes and procedures to reestablish the fact that she was alive and to officially annul her death certificate. In the process she and her parents realized it wasn't easy at all. By the time they were heading to the courtroom, she was at the point of giving up and opting to stay dead if she could. The problem was, staying dead on paper would have denied her so many services, and she just had to keep up with the schedules and get things reversed. It was like being reborn a second time, except this time she wasn't a baby anymore.

* * *

At the Mirogoj Cemetery a crowd of people gathered for a second time at the same tomb for a purpose that happened so rarely in life, and that was astonishingly the first time on the holy grounds of Mirogoj since its establishment on November 6, 1876, a once-in-a-lifetime thing. They removed the casket from the ground to seal her reincarnation ceremony and process. Friends and relatives danced, ululated and jubilated as though they were a bunch of soldiers who'd just conquered a territory. It was a joyous scene for a change in a graveyard.

Having completed the entire process of reestablishing her existence as a "living individual," Matilda was ready for the next phase of her mission. Archibald arrived in Zagreb three weeks after she'd been there battling with the tedious processes with her parents by her side. She picked him up from the railway station in the morning after he arrived from Frankfurt, Germany, having traveled overnight. They spoke for hours, catching up on issues; and once they arrived at her parents' house, she introduced him, and they warmly welcomed him.

She briefly told her story and how they met, keeping it simple and leaving out the complex details of the incredible story about the monsters. She explained a little how they had lived temporarily in isolation in the countryside to explore nature and how she got kidnapped, which consequently hampered her ability to reach out to them for too long. She offered to complete the larger part of the story in the future.

She then mentioned that they got married after she failed to travel back but realized afterward that it wasn't possible for her to explain it to them in a way that they would ever understand on the phone. It was a lot to take in, but her parents had learned to endure, and so they just listened to whatever tale their daughter had to say for the most part.

"For all those reasons, we have to organize a proper marriage-sanctification ceremony that would involve both you my parents and his people," she turned her face to Archibald as she mentioned that. "That also means we're both going back to Alaska to start the process and formally let you guys know what we're going to do and when," she concluded. "I couldn't tell you all that by myself alone. That's why I had to ask him over so he could officially meet you guys face-to-face."

Epilogue

Focus and prioritization turned out to be the fundamental key to Archibald's success as he learned over the years. He was able to win the battle in the jungle because of having one key quality of being "laser" focus. He worked on his weapons-forging for three weeks with undivided attention, and it paid off in the end. He trained and simulated battle scenarios in all kinds of fashions, and that gave him the edge.

When he and Matilda finally left the jungle, they promised each other one thing; they would do their best to rejoin society, assimilate, and catch up with the lost time; but if things didn't spark up to their satisfaction, they were going to leave and go on another voyage, never to return to civilization if possible. The destination was a virgin island almost untouched by man, well, touched but not extensively exploited—the Galapagos Island. And so, after months in their new life, they got themselves jobs: Archibald as a chef in a nearby Mexican Grill while Matilda was working at a flower shop about a mile down the streets from their studio apartment. For Matilda, she had made up her mind if she wasn't going to find work in landscaping that involved interacting with nature, then at least she'd rather sell flowers. And luckily, she got it. At least she could smell the flowers, and that reminded her of all the beautiful time they'd had at the riverside.

Gossiper also adjusted to the slow-paced life but mostly slept due to little to do, and it was an entirely new and hard chapter in his *dog life*. All his life he was raised in the jungle, and so the quietness and especially the redundancy was boring and sickening day in and day out. Archibald did the best he could to diligently walk him every evening after work. At least that helped a bit for the purpose of stretching the muscles and exercising.

Another part of their agreement was to try not to conceive a baby in order not to complicate their plan in case they decided to leave. They didn't want their time of probation to be influenced by a baby on the way. Six months later they had made their firm decision. They were of another world. And so they would leave the Anchorage. It seemed from the time they set foot in the jungle for that extended second date, they were never going back from the life of adventure. And so they laid out their plan in meticulous detail.

They were going to build a twenty-five-by-ten-yard yacht, tough, durable and set sail, never to return to civilization. They hoped to find a new world and raise a generation of their own. But that was a huge responsibility on their shoulders. The resolution meant they were going to laser focus all their attention, savings, time, and preparation for the impending journey into the unknown. By estimate, they needed approximately two and half years to put things together. They decided on a design that would allow for easy transportation down to Susitna River through which they planned to sail out, emerging from its delta into the open Gulf of Mexico, and then into the open sea, the great Pacific Ocean. From there they would set sail to the island of dreams, the adventurer's paradise—Galapagos.

With all the plans laid out on the table, they asked Mr. Doolittle to look into it and give or take out any ideas. Wasting no time, Mr. Doolittle pored through the blueprint of the journey and every headline and examined through the nitty-gritty details. The items to consider included supplies, construction of the yacht, survival kits and tips, weapons and defense, clothes, beverages, protective gears, medicines, finance, traveling route and navigational issues, documentation, construction, seeds and live animals to be propagated while on the island after arrival and so forth. All of those key words had their details in depths as though they were planning a trip to another galaxy.

Even though Archie and Matilda lived in their own apartment, they had dinner together three times a week with Mr. Doolittle to further discuss the sticking issues in the ongoing preparation. It was in one of those discussions that they figured out a way of cutting back on the prep time for the journey from the initial two and half years of waiting due to financial constraints.

Mr. Doolittle argued that if they could work on a proposal, scientific in nature, and modify their journey as though it was a scientific expedition aiming at collecting data as part of a research project to help better understanding of the effects of man's intervention and activities in relation to time as compared to a fairly undisturbed environment, they could attract funding. With that plan, they would set Galapagos Island as a "control quadrant" and a component part of the research from where the vast experimentations were to be undertaken.

If they could cook it up and get some corporations interested, and they actually agree to do the work and later figure out a way of shipping back their findings in a space of three to five years, perhaps they could secure funding to construct the yacht in no time. That was the plan, simple and to the point.

The other option was to generate enthusiasm among adventure-loving folks, well-wishers, and friends in and around the territory and garner a fundraising effort. Archibald preferred the second option, which would shield them off from potential litigation in the event the voyage didn't turn out the way expected.

Besides, designing a scientific research proposal was a head cracker requiring a lot of technicalities and criteria to be adhered to and followed, which he wasn't ready for. Within a week donations, pledges, and contributions started coming in. They made little brochures and leaflets, which were circulated around their streets, churches, and cathedrals. For five months, they had enough money for the construction and all kinds of resources to set sail, but now the challenge was, the pace of the construction could not be hurried beyond the normal pace to allow for a good finish and fortification of the *Galapagos Express*, as they named the yacht. Archie and Mat kept their jobs to supplement whatever they already had and to leave some savings in their bank accounts just in case.

Galapagos Express was twenty meters by six and with a single story, wide at the base and with three luxurious cabins and living quarters. The deck extended about fifteen meters high. The work progressed steadily until late 1951 through the fall, and their target departure date was somewhere late winter at the edge of spring around about March of the following year. That mild winter day, March 12, 1952, down the road a giant trailer pulled the magnificent work, *The Galapagos Express*, and hurled it to sea in a quest to explore and adventure. Two lovebirds, Archie and Matilda, represented the spirit of a small community in the outskirts of Anchorage City to sail to the unknown. They set sail, flying the

United States flag alongside the Alaskan one that danced in the wind as though to give their approval on behalf of the state and the entire nation. Von Voyage was the sign that many in the crowd of onlookers held in their hands as they finally undocked and started their journey into the unknown, disappearing gradually and forever in the distance.

* * *

Finally, the fascination had to come to a halt. It was a Thursday evening when Stephen Logan wrapped up the story he'd been telling his son for a while. They had been chipping at it little by little for almost a full month until that day.

"So when Archibald and Matilda set sail to Galapagos, what happened then?" Larry had asked his father as they enjoyed dinner in their favorite restaurant.

His father could see the anxiety and queries written all over his son's face as he pondered over what could have happened to the couple while in the distant, virgin island.

"Come on, son, don't take it too seriously," he cheered his son, who had seemingly taken the story too deeply at heart. "Let's just say we'll have a continuation about that in the next big story. Whatever happened in Galapagos, you'll be told, I promise. With that said, may I ask you to finish your dinner, son?"

Logan urged him to clear his plate. With everything done, he paid the bill, and Mrs. Sylvia Logan fished a couple of dollar bills from her brown leather purse and placed them on the table for the waiter who had served them, and they rose up and walked out of the restaurant. After they buckled up in their seats, the family car sped off out of the parking lot down the street on their way home for the night.

The End

About the Author

Dennis Obong Awoii was born and raised in Lira, Northern Uganda. He went to Lira Primary/Elementary School, Lango College, Doctor Obote College Boroboro, and Kyambogo University, Kampala-Uganda.

He came to the United States through the DV lottery program during the Obama years and went on to study at National American University in Tulsa, Oklahoma, where he lives with his family.

About *The Devil in the Cave*: in 2018 when their daughter, Kaitlyn, was born, Dennis found himself facing the reality of having to tell her bedtime stories even though she was still very little. That was when he started thinking of writing for her a story in a quest of being counted as a good dad. But he had to put off the idea since he was working on a political book, which required his full attention.

In March 2019 when Dennis saw an advert about a story-writing competition posted on the Tulsa library website where he did his research and writing, he was prompted to start on a simple chapter as a response, since the progress on his other book had stalled as it required a lot of traveling and interviews to continue and complete. The simple chapter of the story Dennis started progressed steadily and became this book, which he decided to publish and share with the world. Dennis hopes to keep the first printed copy for their little girl to read for herself when she becomes of age.

CPSIA information can be obtained
at www.ICGtesting.com
Printed in the USA
LVHW070159160622
721414LV00008B/256